A SAVAGE BREED

PATRICK C. HARRISON III

DEATH'S HEAD PRESS
an imprint of Dead Sky Publishing, LLC

Miami Beach, Florida
www.deadskypublishing.com

ISBN: 9781639510443

Cover Art: Justin T. Coons

The "Splatter Western" logo designed
by K. Trap Jones

Book Layout: Lori Michelle
www.TheAuthorsAlley.com

For Grandad

PROLOGUE:

BITTER AT DAWN

1

THERE WAS TO be no public hanging for the Tate Gang.

No gathering of townsfolk and newspapermen. No shouts of heroism by those who had roused them from slumber after a night of drink and whores. No mention of collecting bounties from Texas and Mexico and God only knew where else.

Six of them stood with their hands bound behind their backs and holes dug in the dirt at their heels. The wind whistled, sending sharp dust into unshielded eyes and setting dead Indiangrass dancing around their legs.

Crow stood at one end of the death-sentenced six, his beard, scraggly and sun-lightened, blowing beneath his sharp, creased face. His hands balled in tight fists beneath the cut lariat that tied his wrists behind his lanky frame.

To his left was Connor, the Irishman, with a drinker's belly that gave away his heritage as much as his red mustache. Beyond him were the three brothers Tate, rugged and unforgiving and hard as granite. And beyond them was the woman who had got them caught, her hair and eyes as dark as a gunfighter's soul.

Morning sun peeked over the low hills to the east, casting long shadows, the Wichita Mountains stretching to the north and west. Baby mountains, to Crow, who had seen the great Rockies in his travels. He had been a prospector in those days and a fur trader. He had been a blacksmith in St. Louis, and worked the whiskey boats on the Mississippi. And now a bank robber and horse thief. All a means to an end; every man's occupation carried its dangers.

Howling gusts blew the Irishman's hat off and stole the sheriff's voice away like a thief as he read the sentencing from atop a big white Andalusian. Even had the lawman not been flanked by six deputies with rifles, the six long, deep holes at their heels made the verdict clear enough.

"I ain't heard a shittin' thing you said, Sheriff," said Dom, the eldest Tate. He spat into the dirt and shook his head.

"Goddamnit!" the sheriff hollered. "You boys and yer injun gal know damn well what I said. Yer sentenced to death, all six of ya, by order of Judge Milo Stanton."

"We ain't had no trial!" Richard, the youngest Tate, said.

"Shut your yammering, boy! We's got other business to tend in Barrier Ridge than the thievin' likes of you. We'll make it quick, don't you be worryin'. Fellas, rifles at the ready."

Barrier Ridge, Crow thought as the deputy in front of him raised his Rolling Block. *I like that name.* Past the man with his rifle, the deputies' horses were tethered loosely to a log in the grass. Past the horses, the terrain sloped upwards to the town, with its three saloons, two general stores, two blacksmiths, two doctors, and one bank that never got robbed by the Tate Gang. And past the town were the mountains, their sand-colored rocks gleaming like peaks of fire in the early light. The mountains swung around the town like a horseshoe, the larger, rockier cliffs to Crow's left and the rolling hills to his right. *Barrier Ridge*, he thought again, before the first trigger was pulled. *I'm gonna die at Barrier Ridge. Not a bad place to call it quits.*

"President Garfield gon skin yor ass for ignoring the Constitution an not givin' us fair trial!" Richard blared as the sheriff called 'Ready!' and the deputies pulled back the hammers on their Remingtons and Winchesters.

"Garfield been dead three months, you twit," the sheriff said. "Aim!"

Crow noticed the cemetery to the east, the crosses and gravestones silhouetted against the hills and sliver of rising sun. *Guess we ain't worthy of the Barrier Ridge graveyard*, he thought. *All the same, to me. The view is better here, I reckon.* The size of the cemetery struck Crow as strange, just as the carrying out of their execution did. Mighty large for a small town. But what did he know? Barrier Ridge may have been one of the oldest American settlements, with a hundred years or more of dropping people in the dirt under God's cross.

"Die, you son of a bitch!"

It was the middle Tate, Noel, who hollered.

The exclamation actually drew Crow's attention away from the mountains (the rifle pointed at his face had somehow failed to do this) and caused him to raise an eyebrow with surprise and curiosity. *A bit late to be picking a fight*, he thought. But he was wrong.

He looked over at the Tates just in time to see the ropes that had been binding their wrists falling to the ground, their arms swinging around in unison, each brother holding a double barrel derringer in each hand. Before Noel fired the first shot, Crow had time to wonder just where in the hell they had been hiding those guns. But then his ears were ringing with gunfire.

The back of Sheriff Hughes' head burst like a dropped egg, his blood and brain matter catching in the wind like a cloud and showering both his horse and the rifle-wielding deputy who stood next to him. The startled horse needed no command to get moving; it hightailed it towards Barrier Ridge with the dead sheriff still in the saddle. The blood-covered deputy, looking shocked and afraid, was the next to go down as Noel stepped forward and plugged him in the chest.

Richard dropped to one knee as another deputy fired his rifle uselessly a foot over his head. His first shot missed the deputy—derringers were famously inaccurate—but the one in his other hand got him, blowing a hole through his left eye.

Dom threw himself flat, unloading both derringers at once, taking out the knee of one deputy and hitting another in the crotch. One of the latter's fleshy testicles fell through the bloody hole in his trousers and plopped atop a small ant hill. The ants responded with predictable ferocity.

All this happened in the split second it had taken Crow to look to his left.

A SAVAGE BREED

If Sheriff Rutherford Hughes had taken the time to familiarize himself with the past exploits of the Tate brothers, he likely would have been a bit more cautious in how he carried out their sentencing.

The Tates had spent their youth traveling back and forth between New York, Boston and Philadelphia with their father's magic show. Tate the Great, he called himself. He would call upon lads and ladies from the audience to bind him in rope or wrap him in chains or lock him in a box, and then, to the wonderment of the crowd, he would escape. Perhaps his greatest escape occurred in 1865, when he was wrapped in chains, which were fastened with four padlocks, then dropped into the Hudson River. In sixty seconds exactly, with a crowd of over 300 spectators growing ever more worried, he surfaced with all four heavy locks in his hands. "I lost the chain," *The New York Times* reported him saying, "but damned if I was going to lose four good locks."

Consequently, Tate the Great's three boys grew up learning how to free themselves from all manner of things, from simple ties, to handcuffs and even jail cells. When, in their teens and early twenties, Dom, Noel, and Richard decided to head west and pursue their riches by way of the gun, it was with full knowledge that if detained by the law, they wouldn't be detained long.

Had Sheriff Hughes done his homework, he would know that the Tate brothers had escaped imprisonment in San Antonio, Fort Worth and El Paso, gunning down three lawmen and two civilians in the process. He would know that tying a Tate's wrists together was no different than leaving him unrestrained. But Sheriff Hughes had been ignorant to this information.

Crow himself, while not ignorant to it, had certainly underestimated the brothers.

When he whipped his head forward again, wide-eyed and with a renewed desire to live, seeming to see things in slow motion, he saw the Remington Rolling Block still aimed as his head and the trigger being compressed. All he could think to do was fall backwards, his hands still bound together at his ass. The rifle cracked and the bullet tore through the wide, flat brim of Crow's hat (a nice black hat he had won gambling in Dodge City). He landed painfully in the hard, cold grave that was meant for his corpse.

He's got to reload, Crow thought frantically, not recalling a revolver on the man's hip. *I've got to move!* For a panicked half-second he rolled and wriggled like a June bug stuck on its backside. But then he jerked himself to a sitting position and fought quickly to his feet. Luckily, though the hole had felt ten feet deep when he collided with the ground, jarring his skull and sending sharp pains up his arms, it was no more than two. Crow, seeing the deputy loading another round into the rifle, jumped from the hole, his boots catching on the edge and slipping on loose terrain. His body flailed forward and once again his bound arms were unable to brace his fall. His chest and face thudded against the dirt, a jagged stone striking his right cheek, sending piercing warm pain through that side. Spitting blood and grit from his mouth, Crow struggled back to his feet.

Gunshots rang. Not the snaps of derringers, their loads had been spent, but the booming, more authoritative reports of rifles and high-caliber revolvers. And there was shouting. "Kill 'em all!" and "Get the squaw!" and "Grab the horses!" The Irishman was yelling, "you bloody cock-sucking bastard!" But Crow heard none of it with any relative comprehension. Nor did he witness the action going on about him. He only saw the breach of the Remington being rolled closed and the hammer being cocked back.

Crow charged, screaming like a wild Apache, blood dripping from his mouth and cheek. His hat, crumpled and bullet-shot, flew from his head. The deputy pulled the rifle up, but Crow avoided it, cutting to one side, then lowering his head and plowing into the man like an angry bull charging a matador, He felt the deputy's ribs crack beneath the impact of his skull and heard his breathless yelp like an injured dog. They both went down. For the third time in a matter of seconds, Crow fought to get himself off the ground before someone put a bullet in him.

He got to his side and pushed himself up on an elbow. The deputy, lying on his back, had pain painted on his face, but wasn't about to let that get in the way of his executionary duties. He brought the rifle around as Crow once again jumped forward. His body struck the Remington broadside as it went off, the blast roaring less than inch from Crow's ear, the bullet shaving a few long strands of hair from his head.

With his head ringing like a bell tower, Crow straddled the man and, still without use of his hands, mounted the only attack he could think of. He bent down, put his mouth around the deputy's nose, and bit down hard. The man screamed, releasing the rifle, clawing wildly at Crow's shirt and body. But Crow only bit harder, clenching his teeth so tight together that his jaw bones ached. He twisted on the nose, blood spewing into his mouth, the deputy's screams becoming gargled as more blood poured down his throat. The deputy's hands dug into Crow's side, his fingernails puncturing flesh and ripping skin. But Crow held on.

Then the deputy's head was blown to the side in a mess of blood, bones, and brain. The nose tore loose in Crow's mouth. Crow sat up, looking first at the noseless deputy with half his skull missing, then around him, his face dripping with gore.

"Jesus Christ, Crow," Richard Tate said, laughing. Noel stood beside him with a smoking lever action in his hands. "You didn't get enough prairie dog for dinner last night?"

"Saddle up dem horses, boys," Dom said, coming alongside his brothers and looking down at Crow without reaction. "We need to make dem mountains before sundown." He nodded to the west.

"We need to catch our squaw first," Noel said, nodding to the south, where the woman was running with hands still tied behind her.

Connor, spewing an incoherent assembly of heavily accented profanity, appeared beside the brothers, bleeding from his right shoulder and toting a Colt revolver. As he placed his retrieved bowler hat on his curly red head, he looked at Crow. "Christ, man, the blazes happened to you?"

Crow stood slowly, wavering a little in the stiff wind, and spat the deputy's nose out. "Somebody untie me," he said.

2

THE **SHOVEL HAD** broken before he was halfway done, so James Haggard dug with his hands until they bled, and buried his wife and daughter with the sun creeping over the horizon.

It was colder in the mountains than it was two miles south in Barrier Ridge. A thin layer of frost gleamed like jewels. Meredith would have found it pretty and asked if it was going to snow. Sarah would have stoked the fire and got some water boiling for coffee. But never again.

Haggard stood over the mounds of dirt and rock beneath which he had lain the mangled bodies of his family. With cold tears on his cheeks, he recited what he could of the Lord's prayer. "Amen," he muttered at its conclusion, closing his eyes and remembering their faces, their blonde hair and soft skin, the hug of his daughter and the kiss of his wife. His legs gave way and he fell to his knees sobbing, placing a hand atop each grave. "Why?" he said. "Why them?"

He fell forward and curled up between his buried wife and daughter, tucking his cold and raw hands beneath his arms, shivering. Almost instantly, and completely unintended, he fell asleep, his body drained from the previous day's adventures, and the horrors that met his arrival back home.

He had left the previous morning with his horse, Robert (named after Haggard's father), and his Winchester lever-action, hoping to spook a coyote or a deer—maybe even a turkey—and bring it home for dinner. He headed east towards the hills (the rocks to the west offered little more than mountain lions and bobcats and evasive small fowl), but had traveled several miles without seeing so much as fresh track in the dirt. Around noon he took a squat on a flat stone on a ridge overlooking the prairie and drank water from his leather canteen, and chewed on a lime that Sarah bought with a half dozen other fruits in Barrier Ridge two weeks prior. His eyes grew heavy as he gazed down on the rolling plains, and he'd been on the verge of dozing when Robert woke him, likely saving his life.

The old horse had been waiting patiently, as he always did, when Haggard sat down to rest. So, when Robert brayed like a mare in heat, Haggard jolted upright and grabbed at his gun, which was leaned against a nearby rock.

The sound of pounding earth and rock grew loud behind him as his hand closed around the blue steel of the Winchester, and he knew without seeing it what was coming. He spun, pulling down the hammer as he did so, and yanked back the trigger, his eyes seeing nothing but a mass of dark fur.

The bullet tore through the side of the black bear's neck. It wasn't enough to drop the beast, but it caused the bear to jerk to the left with its final stride, missing its intended target—Haggard—by less than an inch, actually knocking his hat off as it soared past. Robert was not so lucky. The startled horse, whose final act was a heroic one, stood by his master's side even as the bear was upon him. When it veered to the left, it veered into Robert, crashing into him with claws out and teeth bared. Helplessly, Haggard watched the two animals topple and roll, hearing Robert's ribs crack and the wild painful cries of them both. And then they were gone, over the edge and down the sloping rock towards the rolling hills below.

"No!" Haggard yelled, stumbling forward, his arm outstretched, nearly going over himself. He watched the horse named Robert descend until he came to a final bloody stop at the base of the mountain, back twisted awkwardly around the trunk of a blackjack oak. The horse he had had for six years. The saddle, even longer.

After a good-long yell of disapproval, Haggard got to his feet, strapped the rifle and canteen across his back, and began the long, horseless trek home. It was likely there were cubs in the area, given the black bear's behavior, but he did not search for them.

Nightfall had long since arrived by the time he'd reached the cabin, the halfmoon bright between the clouds of an overcast sky, a cold Oklahoma wind whipping around the mountains. The fire in the fireplace had dwindled to embers and no lanterns burned.

And his wife and daughter, their arms still entangled as if in a warm embrace, lay butchered and broken in the cabin's far corner. Sarah still clutched a knife in one dead hand. Meredith's bloodstained handkerchief doll hung at the end of her limp fingers.

Only moments after his eyes closed, the sound of distant gunshots woke him from his nightmarish memories. They sounded miles away, in Barrier Ridge, perhaps, or even further. It was hard to tell with the wind. Haggard didn't find this too unusual. Barrier Ridge seemed to attract gunfights and death. At least, that's how it seemed from his perch in the mountains, where he often heard the blasts of rifles and revolvers, even in the middle of the night.

"Indians," Haggard said, pushing himself up, wiping gravel from his coat and britches. "Goddamn Comanche."

It was them who had murdered his wife and daughter, there was no doubt. Haggard had heard stories of wild Comanche—the savages!—in the area, killing men for no better reason than being on what they considered their land. He'd heard the horrifying tales of women being raped and children thrown amongst hungry wolves.

And he knew where their nearest camp was. He'd passed the camp, just over a mile away, on his travels to the west through the mountains. It was a small group of Indians—between twelve and fifteen, he thought. It would be a lot less before this morning was over. He had no way of knowing if the killer, or killers, had come from there. But the deed had surely been the work of Comanche, and he would have his revenge.

Haggard saddled Meredith's pony, the one she had gotten for her fifth birthday three years ago, the only horse he had left. Then he loaded his Winchester and his revolver, strapping the former to his back and the latter to his hip. He put more cartridges in the loops on his belt and the bandolier across his chest. Using one of Sarah's sewing needles, he pinned Meredith's bloodstained handkerchief doll to his coat.

He mounted the pony and kissed the head of the handkerchief doll, then kissed his wedding band. Bitter wind whirled around him. Dawn had arrived and Hell wasn't far behind.

3

ELIZABETH HUGHES WAS milking the cows when Lightning, her father's pearly white Andalusian, ambled into the barn, then into its stall as if no greater event had occurred than a blustery pleasure-ride across the prairie. Hearing the horse's movement, Elizabeth, sitting beneath a cow and with her hand still on the teat, turned. Lifting her bonnet, she saw her father's boot between the wood boards.

"Well, you're back earlier than expected, Papa," she said, returning to her duties of filling the pail with milk. "Did you not get enough to eat this morning? I would have made more, but . . . well, you know how Momma is."

He *did* know how Momma was. He had told Elizabeth so. Momma was fearful. Fearful they would run out of food, fearful they would run out of water, fearful that Papa would get gunned down by some outlaw, fearful the Comanches would scalp them all (Elizabeth had never heard of the Comanche scalping anyone, but you didn't question Momma), fearful about what Elizabeth had done to that Mosely boy and his dog, and, most of all, fearful of the mountains. She had good reason to be afraid of the mountains, so she told Elizabeth and everyone else that would listen.

Momma had lost her entire family on an expedition through the Wichita Mountains. Only she, at the tender age of ten, had escaped to the little town of Barrier Ridge. And in the thirty-three years since, she had not left the prairie.

"I heard a lot of shootin' this morning," Elizabeth said, undeterred by her Papa's silence. She was a talkative fifteen-year-old and was okay with people just a-sittin' and a-listenin'. "I guess y'all really put it to those bandits."

Elizabeth twisted the cow's teat in her fingers until it turned red, a dribble of milk clinging to its tip like sweat on the end of your nose. The cow stammered uncomfortably, and Elizabeth smiled and released it.

"Papa, ain't you gonna tell me about killing them boys? You know I like to hear about it. I ain't scared to listen, like Momma is. And what about the squaw? Did you kill her too? Did she . . . " She paused, biting her lip and grinning, then continued. "Was she violated by those men?" Then, quietly, almost a whisper, she said, "How many do you think had their way with her?"

Elizabeth, still crouched beneath the dairy cow, waited, her patience growing thin. Momma wouldn't stand for such crass questions, but Papa understood her a little better. It wasn't just the incident with the pigs—which was completely overblown, in Elizabeth's opinion—or how Papa had been the one to find her after that whole mess with the whore and the barkeep; it was that, being a lawman, Papa understood what people were capable of, and understood that some people, Elizabeth included, were *different*.

Lightning shifted nervously in her stall, but her father made not a peep. Elizabeth sighed and spat into the pail of milk and looked through the boards again, at the lower half of the horse and her father's boot.

That was when she saw the blood. A single trail of blood, looking like a stream of red, ran down the white coat of Lightning's shoulder, cut across her ribs, and dripped onto the polished black of her father's boot.

Bolting from her spot beneath the cow, Elizabeth ran around the wooden barriers that separated her from Sheriff Rutherford Hughes, the respected and feared lawman, and father of the detested but possibly just as feared Elizabeth.

Papa was dead, slumped over the beautiful Andalusian with his blood peppering its snowy coat, and a hole the size of a fist in the back of his head.

"Son-of-a-bitch," Elizabeth said, her hands on her hips. "Well, you sure fucked up right good, didn't you? And I suppose you're expecting me to give you a proper Christian burial, too. Well, that ain't happening, I'll tell you that now."

She grabbed hold of the sheriff's belt and yanked on him, his body tilting to one side but refusing to come off the horse. "Get your foot outta the goddamn stirrup, Papa. Geez!" When she dislodged his boot from it, his obese body collapsed heavily amongst the hay and horse shit, a pool of blood and brain matter forming beneath his head.

"Momma can take care of all that funeral business," Elizabeth said, looking her father square in the leaking hole in his head. "I reckon she'll do good.

I sure as hell ain't sticking around Barrier Ridge with you deader than Abe Lincoln. The town folk would have me swinging from the trees like a runaway slave in no time."

She bent down and removed her father's Colt revolver from its holster. The front sight snagged on a yellowed, folded piece of paper tucked inside his belt, pulling it loose and halfway unfolded before it fell to the hay. Elizabeth slid the revolver into the belt around the waist of her dress, then retrieved and opened the paper. It was a "Wanted" poster, she saw, for some ugly brute.

"Don't reckon you'll be tracking down this outlaw, Papa. Good job getting killed. This Black Magpie—whoever the devil that is—doesn't have to worry about you no more. It probably would've behooved you to have this here Colt in your hand instead of your holster if you planned on killing some bandits today. But what do I know? I'm just a kid; you're the sheriff."

Tossing the "Wanted" poster to the ground, Elizabeth grabbed the reins around Lightning's neck and led her out of the barn. The harsh morning wind whipped at her dress and bonnet as she walked towards the house, where she tied the horse to a post on the porch and went inside. Passing her mother, who sat silently in a rocking chair knitting a scarf for Papa that he would never use, Elizabeth put the revolver aside to shed her dress and bonnet She stood in nothing more than her pantaloons while she sifted through her wooden chest of clothing and blankets, her budding breasts sharp from the cold.

"What in the name of the good Lord are you doing?" Momma snapped, the scarf falling to her lap.

"Cover yourself, Elizabeth Grace! Lord, have mercy on this child. And where were you yesterday evening? You missed dinner and didn't put the chickens back in the coop."

"Papa is dead and I am leaving," Elizabeth said, pulling on a pair of wool trousers. "I ain't staying here."

"What?" Momma said, her eyes suddenly wide with worry. "What do you mean, your Pa is dead? He most certainly is not!"

"The hell he ain't. Go out to the barn and have a look for yourself." She donned a flannel shirt and wide-brimmed hat, then secured a belt with a holster around her waist and dropped the Colt into place.

"Elizabeth, I am not going to listen to your lies. Father Milton told you that's a sin and—"

"All Father Milton cares about is whiskey and whores, so you save me your little lecture about anything he says, Momma. And I ain't lying. Go look for yourself. You got legs."

"What . . . " Momma started, looking from Elizabeth to the front door, then back again. "Your Pa is really dead?"

"For the fiftieth time, yes," Elizabeth said, pulling worn leather boots onto her feet.

Momma stood, the scarf falling from her lap to the floor, her lips quivering. Her eyes were on the revolver at Elizabeth's hip. This—seeing Rutherford Hughes's gun in possession of his daughter—seemed to cement the truth for her. "Wha . . . what did you do to him?"

"I didn't do nothing to him," Elizabeth said, now taking the gleaming Henry rifle off the wall and loading it.

"You're lying!"

Elizabeth turned and looked at her mother as she injected another round into the rifle. "I ain't lying. If I was gonna kill one of my parents, you really think it would be Papa?"

Momma gasped, hands going to her chest as if she were punched there.

"I'm taking that bread I baked earlier. You don't need it, you're filling out your midsection right well already. And I'll take that scarf too. And I'm taking Lightning. You would let her legs grow old and weak, if I left her."

"Where are you going, Elizabeth? You can't leave me here alone!" Momma's voice broke with tearless sobs. She was getting hysterical, as Momma often did.

"I don't know. Away from you. Reckon I'll head west, maybe to California."

"California? No, Elizabeth! I forbid it! There's nothing but drunks and outlaws in California! And chinks!"

"Well, that sounds exciting. Whatever a chink is."

"No! Goddamnit, Elizabeth!"

"Taking the Lord's name in vain, Momma? Father Milton would be right disappointed in you." The Henry rifle slung across her back, she loaded a leather satchel with her favorite Bowie knife, ammo, matches, the scarf and dress, and the bread.

"Don't leave me here alone, Elizabeth! You'll die if you go west! If you set foot in those mountains, you will die! You don't know what's out there!"

"I know what's out there: wind and Indians and a whole lot of lies and superstitions. I ain't scared of none of it. I ain't like you. Goodbye, Momma, you old hag."

PART ONE:

THE TATE GANG

1

HAVING PILLAGED THE belongings of the downed deputies and rode off on their horses, the Tate Gang reached the mountains by sundown. They set up camp in the foothills, dining on prairie dogs and rabbits for dinner, having their way with the squaw before bedding down beneath wool blankets, with the wind howling and the campfire's flames flickering erratically between dry logs.

"You're up, Crow," Noel said, buttoning his britches and looking across the fire at him. He slapped her ass and threw the blanket over her. She was crying. "Her cunt ain't too bad. Best you poke it before it freezes shut."

Crow wrapped his own blanket around him and inched closer to the fire. Coyotes howled with the wind. The mountains loomed in the moonlight. Connor's snores were so loud that they seemed to echo off the rocks. It didn't seem to bother Richard or Dom, who were both sleeping soundly after having their fill of the squaw. Crow would have done anything for a glass of whiskey right then.

"Crow?" Noel snapped.

"Ain't interested tonight," Crow said. "Too cold and too tired."

"Suit yourself." Noel shoved the squaw, telling her to make room for him by the fire.

Doing as she was told, she cinched the blanket around her head and body. Crow could see the reflection of flames in her wet eyes. Her blanket shivered, and Crow figured her tremors were as much from fear and shame as cold. It was his fault she was here. *I should have put a bullet in her when I had the chance*, he thought. As if on cue, a single report of rifle fire sounded and echoed through the hills. It came from two or three miles to the east, Crow guessed— far enough away for him to know the shot wasn't aimed at them, but too close for comfort. Noel seemed not to notice as he warmed his hands, and nary one of the rest of the gang stirred in their sleep. So, Crow just picked a piece of grass from the earth and stuck it between his teeth, and thought on how it'd all come to this.

The Tate Gang had been making their way west after robbing two small, but lucrative banks in Tyler, Texas, at first following the Sabine River, but eventually having to make their way into the thick woods when it became clear that Rangers were on their tail and moving fast. That was when they got lost. They had only been off the river for a day when a band of Mexicans made off with their horses and half their loot in the night.

Dom, the unelected leader of the group, was determined to track down the thieves, but it soon became clear that the woods were damn near impossible to navigate. The forests of East Texas were not like those of the Rockies, Crow discovered; they were thick with brush and thorn bushes and ant hills, and the trees had limbs like whips that were torturous to the skin and difficult to set ablaze. Movement was slow and overcast skies made the gang disoriented. Before long, tempers flared and they argued over direction and flung blame at each other over their situation and the loss of their horses. At one point, Richard and Noel pulled their revolvers on each other while Dom encouraged them to pull the trigger. Connor had found this quite funny.

Meanwhile, Crow, who, although now a bank robber, was never allured by confrontation, was considering making off through the woods on his own. He was hungry and exhausted and just as lost as the rest of them. Perhaps he could do better on his own. At the very least, if he came across an armadillo, he wouldn't have to share it with the other four men.

Then they'd smelled the smoke. Drizzle had hampered their ability to make fires in the days since leaving the river, and the lack of food or optimism kept them from trying for more than a few minutes. But the smell of fire roused their spirits and the rumble of their stomachs. And the sounds of Spanish conversation had the Tates thirsty for blood.

2

A **LIGHT RAIN** had started as the five-man Tate Gang quietly made their approach to the camp of Mexican horse thieves. They crawled on their bellies as they drew near, and Crow was thankful for the rain which quieted the rustle of leaves. They huddled behind a giant downed oak tree and peered through its rotten branches. Crudely constructed lean-tos flanked a large fire, at least a dozen men were crowded beneath them. Bound in rope, two Indian women shivered beneath a tree beyond the fire. Numerous horses were tied to the trees behind them. A man was leading one horse to the center of the camp, with two other men following him.

"That's my horse," Richard whispered. "Those thieving sons of bitches got my horse."

"You stole that horse in Shreveport," Connor said, holding his hand over his mouth to suppress laughter.

"Shut up, you stupid Irish bastard. Dom, let's get down there and grab our horses."

"Now hold on," Dom said, placing his hand on his brother's arm to keep him from standing. "We're outnumbered and probably outgunned. Let's wait 'til they're down for the night. Then we'll get our horses and some food too. If we have to pull steel on 'em, then we will. But I ain't running down there guns blazing in the daylight over your ugly-ass horse."

"We can take them bastards," Richard hissed between gritted teeth, but he didn't move. He seemed content to wait for nightfall.

The five men settled behind the downed tree, wrapped in their coats and shivering as much as the Indian women at the camp. Crow's eyes closed and he tried to ignore his rumbling stomach and damp clothes. He wasn't sure they could take on the Mexican thieves and survive, especially since only one of the Tate Gang had a rifle, but he was willing to try if it meant getting food in his belly. He had only an elementary understanding of Spanish, and most of what conversations he could hear meant nothing to him, until one phrase came through clear and made his eyes snap open: "Mata al caballo!"

Kill the horse!

Crow turned and peered over the log just in time to see one of the thieves pressing the barrel of his revolver against the horse's head. *What the hell are they doing?* Crow thought. *And please, God in Heaven, let Richard stay calm.* The man holding the gun pulled the trigger and the sound it made echoed through the woods. The head split in two and blood sprayed out the other side, the horse—a tall, muscular quarter horse—instantly falling over. One of the men had been standing to the rear side of the horse, and when it fell, his legs were crushed beneath it. Crow heard the fracture of bone, followed by his screams, the horse spasming atop him as life seeped from it.

But it wasn't the screams of the injured Mexican that worried Crow; the reaction of Richard Tate was what worried him. It didn't take but a split second to discover which direction that wind was blowing.

"What in the hell!" Richard jumped to his feet with his revolver pulled. "He shot my fuckin' horse!"

"Damn it, Rich!" Dom said, removing his own Colt from its holster. "Let's go boys. Dickhead decided to start this party early."

Fuck, Crow thought, *I should have stayed on the goddamn whiskey boats.* Reluctantly, he unholstered his revolver and pulled the hammer to the rear.

"Christ Almighty, Rich, ya dumb bastard!" Connor said, slinging his Henry rifle off his back. Kneeling and propping the Henry on the large downed oak, Connor added, "I won't be going down there with you fellas. Keep outta my way and let me blast the devils!"

But the Tates were already barreling towards the camp with guns blazing. The man who had led the horse to the center of camp was first to go down, followed closely by the man that killed the horse. Crow hesitated, looking at Connor with gritted teeth and furious eyes. He wasn't much the talkative type, but Connor seemed to understand his stare.

"Go on down there, Crow, and help the boys. I promise not to shoot ya. I may give one to that blasted Richard, though. Nothing but turd flies under that chap's hat. Now, go on before Dom thinks ye're yella."

Crow gave him a sly smile and said, "I ain't yella." And then he was over the tree and sprinting through the weak, misting rain and the haze of gunsmoke.

Dom and Richard were to the right, unloading their guns into the Mexicans beneath the lean-to on that side, most of them young and apparently unarmed. Noel, the only one of them with two revolvers (one a Colt Navy and the other a Colt Army) took the left and blasted a man with a scatter gun in his hands, dropped a kid who couldn't have been more than fourteen who was holding a Bowie knife at his side, then blew a red hole into the back of a sombrero of a guy making his escape.

It appeared the Tates had everything well in hand until a large woman ("She had a mouth like a basking shark, that lady!" is how Connor would describe her later, which none of the American-born men would understand) burst around the end of the lean-to. Screaming insults in Spanish – Crow could swear she was saying something about wanting chickens to peck their dicks – and wielding a large lever action rifle, the woman fired. She was more pointing the gun than aiming, but the first round zipped past Crow's ear.

"Whoa," Crow said under his breath, then leveled his revolver at her and pulled the trigger. He was a good distance away from her and had never claimed to be an expert marksman, but he managed to blow a hole in her left shoulder.

She only screamed louder, lifted the rifle back up, and fired again. This time, the bullet grazed Noel's thigh and he yelled, dropping one of his revolvers and going down to one knee.

"Kill that whore!" he yelled, his own remaining gun making nothing but a lonely, deathly click as he repeatedly pulled back the hammer and pulled the trigger.

Holding his Colt with both hands, Crow took steadier aim as the woman shifted the rifle in his direction again. Gunshots seem to explode all around him. From the right and left and behind. Front in front of him and from his own hand. Simultaneously, Crow, the fat woman, Connor, Noel, having picked his Colt Army up off the ground, and the other two Tates all fired. The result was, the fat lady with the big mouth took five bullets while the wooded hillside behind Crow took only one. She collapsed like a sack of wet beans and her yammering was no more.

Crow blasted a wounded man who was reaching for his pistol. Connor picked off two fleeing through the woods. The Tates commenced plugging the corpses of the men they'd already shot, just to be sure. One of the Indian women, Crow noticed, had been hit during the dispute and lay on the ground, blood dripping from her buckskin tunic to the freezing mud. She didn't appear to be breathing.

But the other—a young squaw with long, wet black hair and big brown eyes—still knelt in the freezing mud, shivering, her buckskin top and cotton trousers soaked through with rain.

"English?" Crow said as he approached her.

She said nothing, only shivering, her bottom lip trembling, and Crow wondered if it was from fear or cold.

"Español?" he said.

Again, the squaw said nothing.

He put the barrel of his revolver to her forehead. "My parents were killed by Indians," he said. "I don't hold it against you. They weren't much the parenting type, anyhow. But this is a harsh world, and I just think you're better off not in it."

It was the most Crow had spoken in two weeks, and the words felt strange and soggy coming out of his mouth. He wondered why he bothered telling the woman what he was doing. *Maybe I'm telling myself,* he thought. He pulled back the hammer.

"Slow your horses, Crow," Dom said from behind him. "Let's keep that'n alive. Maybe she can bandage Noel's leg. And maybe she can cook that horse."

"Cook the horse?" Richard yelled from the other side of camp where he was picking through the pockets of the deceased. "We ain't eating my horse!"

"Rich, you don't know shit from honey, do ya?" Dom said. "They shot your goddamn horse cuz they ain't got no food. If you want to starve, go on and starve. But the rest of us are eating horse."

3

THE **CALICO CALABOOSE** had the best selection of whiskey and whores in Barrier Ridge. So, despite there only being two vacant rooms above the saloon (The Tequila Troth had five empty rooms, but only one fat, old whore), that was where the Tate Gang settled down two weeks after their romp with the Mexican horse bandits.

"I miss the gargles of Ireland," Connor said to Crow, the two of them sitting at the long bar of the Calico Calaboose. "This American whiskey gets me slewed before the stars is even out. I miss the pandy, too. Nothing like an Irish pandy. I hadn't been home in donkey's years, Crow." His eyes were glazed with drunkenness and his speech was slurred, and Crow didn't have a clue what he was talking about.

"The whiskey is alright," Crow said, throwing back another shot.

"There's only forty-six cards in this deck," Noel said from a table where he sat ready to deal cards to Richard and two Barrier Ridge men. "How in the hell are we supposed play a fair game with forty-six goddamn cards?"

"Just deal, saphead," Richard said, throwing back his fifth shot of rye in the last thirty minutes.

"Call me saphead again, you cocksucking bastard."

"Saphead."

"Would you two shut up and play?" Dom said from the bar a couple of seats down from Connor and Crow, where he was reading a six-month old issue of *The San Antonio Express* while smoking old tobacco in a corncob pipe. "Y'all ain't played a fair game of cards since you was kids. So, it don't make no difference how many you got."

The barmaid placed a bowl of beans in front of Connor, and he quickly and loudly began scooping it into his gullet. "It ain't pandy and it ain't stew, but it'll do," he said, with beans dripping down his scruffy red chin.

"Goddamn, you fat Irishman, stop smacking so loud whiles you eat. I'm trying to read the dern paper."

"Damn right," Richard said, "you're disrupting the concentration at the card table."

"He sounds like a fuckin' pig at the trough," said Noel. The other men at the card table laughed.

"You Tates shut your damn yammering," Connor said. "I haven't had a decent meal in weeks. That injun gal you boys decided to drag along can't cook worth a fuck and she's slower about it than a dead turtle. And you can't read, Dom; you're just looking at the pictures, we all know it."

"Where is Whispering Wind, anyway?" Crow asked as bowl of beans was set in front of him, along with a with round of rye. He shoved the beans around with a dirty wooden spoon, noticing chunks of meat that might have been chicken but he didn't think so.

Shoveling the first bite into his mouth, Crow grimaced. The meal needed seasoning in a bad way. "Barmaid, you got any salt?" Both of his questions went unanswered.

"I can so read, you blabbering idiot!" Dom said, looking up from his paper. "In fact, I read how about forty years ago a bunch of crooked Irishmen decided to sail to America because they was too dumb to grow potatoes in their homeland. And my daddy, Tate the Great, told me how them fuckin' Irish squandered all the opportunities New York afforded 'em. The Irish ain't nuthin but drunks and thieves, just like the Indians."

Crow sighed. He had gotten accustomed to nightly verbal altercations within the Gang, and occasional physical ones. The barmaid, a heavy-set, graying woman, crossed her arms in front of her bosom and eyed the men. *She's preparing herself to break up a fight*, Crow thought. "Is this chicken in with the beans?" Crow asked, attempting to draw the woman's attention away from Connor and Dom.

"Possum," she said. "And you boys better settle it down. I won't have no squabbling in my saloon. If you cause a ruckus, you ain't getting no more drinks, and no whores."

"Shut up, wench, and get me another bowl of beans," Connor said. "And Dom, you take that shit back right now before I blow a hole in your head."

"You drunk son-of-a-whore," Richard said, eyeing his hand of cards, "you couldn't shoot a hole in the floor, much less Dom's head."

Dom resumed reading his paper, seemingly unconcerned about Connor, whose face was reddening with anger. The barmaid, scowling, placed another bowl of beans in front of him. "I said settle it down," she said.

"Get me whiskey, too," Connor said. "Two more."

"I ain't giving you no more drinks," the barmaid said. The Tates erupted with laughter at this refusal.

"What?" Connor said, dropping his spoon halfway to his mouth, beans and possum splattering across the bar top. "What the hell do you mean you're not giving me anymore drinks, wench?"

"You heard what I said. You're plumb soused. Don't need no more."

"Where did Whispering Wind go?" Crow asked again. It was all he could think to say in a vain attempt to break the tension.

Connor looked at Crow, his face red and bewildered. "The hell you talking about, Crow?" Then he looked back to the barmaid. "Look, wench, I don't know if you're weak north of the ears or crazy or just a hateful old hag, but you're gonna get me my whiskey or there's gonna be problems." With that, Connor removed his revolver from its holster, pulled back the hammer, and placed it on the bar top with his finger on the trigger and the barrel aimed at the barmaid. "And you'll be next, Dom Tate!"

"Big talk," Dom said, his eyes still scanning the paper without worry.

"Connor, put the gun away," Crow said. "Let's eat our supper and call it a night."

"Bitch," Connor said. "I'll shove this barrel up your cunt and pull the trigger if you don't pour me another drink."

"Water or milk?" the barmaid said, crossing her

arms in front of her again and leaning against the counter to her rear. Crow was shocked to see that the woman was actually smirking at Connor, challenging him to make good on his threats.

Crow hadn't been with the Tate Gang long, but he'd been with them long enough to know that they didn't take to being told 'no' with much enthusiasm. Connor was typically the most subdued of the bunch, other than Crow himself, but once he'd been drinking, well, he was as predictable as the Oklahoma wind. And when the barmaid inquired if he would prefer water or milk, the saloon again erupted in laughter, which didn't service to douse his temper in the least.

"Alright, have it your way," Connor said, lifting the revolver off the bar and pointing it at the barmaid.

Crow's right hand went to his revolver. *Is Dom seriously going to let this happen?* he thought. "Connor," he said, "just put the gun down. We don't need this—"

"Well, hello boys!"

This interruption came from above them—a wood plank staircase rose beside the bar, leading to the series of rooms used for whoring and sleeping the night away. A red-haired woman wearing a tight corset that accentuated her blessedly large bosom leaned over the railing of the second floor, looking down at Connor and Crow and the other patrons. Every swinging dick in the saloon was staring back at her. Four other women emerged behind the redhead, and they too peered down at the men, smiling, their cheeks rosy with makeup and their bodies outfitted in beautiful flowing skirts beneath tight corsets.

A SAVAGE BREED

"Dear god," Dom said, his pipe falling from his mouth, the San Antonio newspaper forgotten.

The card game came to a halt. Connor's revolver was still pointed at the barmaid, but his grip was loose and his eyes were no longer on the intended target. Crow's breathing was heavy and he held a tight yet shaky grip on his gun, which he'd pulled halfway from its holster. He looked from the girls to Connor to the barmaid, who was looking at Connor's gun as if she might snatch it from his grasp at any moment. Crow felt this would be a horrible idea on her part and silently prayed that she wouldn't attempt such a thing.

"Big fella," the redhead said, looking directly at Connor, "why don't you put that silly gun away and come up here with Miss Darlene? I'll get you out of those dirty clothes and wash you up and show you all my secret, sinful tricks."

"I just wanted a shot of whiskey," Connor said, though there was no longer any power in his voice.

"Honey, I'll gladly pour you a drink up here. Just don't let it take the steel out of your barrel, if you know what I mean."

Just like that, the confrontation between Connor and the barmaid was ancient history. As was Dom's criticism of the Irish. The revolver was put away, the short set of cards was put away, and the newspaper was folded and placed at the end of the bar where it had been.

"Let's go, Crow," Connor said, standing up from the bar with a wide smile on his face, looking like a completely different person than he had moments ago. "There's a whore for each of us!"

"I'm gonna finish my beans and possum first," Crow said, then asked for the third time, "Where did Whispering Wind go?"

"Who?" Connor said, barely paying attention as he and the other men made their way to the stairs.

"Our squaw."

"Rich let some priest or man of the cloth take her up to a room. Why, you in the mood for some injun pussy? It's nothing special. Besides, Crow, that bitch is cold as an Irish winter."

"I'll wait, I guess," Crow said, turning his attention back to the bowl of beans.

"You're odder than a two-headed pup, Crow," Connor said, following the Tates to the second floor. "Enjoy your possum. I'm going for dessert."

4

FATHER RONALD MILTON lifted himself off the Indian woman, his body slick with sweat, grabbing his pecker as he did so and smearing the last drop of semen across the squaw's inner thigh. She appeared not to notice. He had poked his share of women, whores—"the temptresses of Satan," as he frequently called them during Sunday morning Mass—being the greatest majority of them, and this squaw, though beautiful, was lively as a dead fish, like most slave women and young girls tended to be. Well-paid whores and adulterous wives were far more exciting.

The woman sobbed, a tear streaking down her cheek in the lantern's glow. Father Milton smiled and wiped the tear from her face, then licked its salty dampness from his finger. From the adjacent rooms he heard the commencement of fornication between whores and the men who'd brought the squaw. They'd been dirty and rugged and hungry, and more than happy to lend him their squaw for ten generous dollars, collected, of course, during Wednesday's evening Mass at St. Peter's Catholic Church.

"God be with you, child," Father Milton said, wiping the sweat from his balding head as he stood. He was naked before her, and she rolled away from him on the bed, facing the window where the faint glow of moonlight snuck through winter clouds like a thief. Feeling his penis shrinking back into his groin, Father Milton tugged on it. "You're a beautiful child of God, but you're cursed with the devil's slit, as all women are. I'm not the first good man to falter in the face of such temptation. And I will have you again before this night is done, and then we will pray. We will pray that God forgives you for possessing that evil pit of pleasure between your legs. We will pray, my child."

The squaw said nothing. But she trembled and Father Milton thought this was good. It was rare that a woman showed him, a man of the cloth, defiance, but it happened on occasion. For these women, prayer was typically a lost cause; he had other ways of getting the message of God across. So, crying was a good thing.

With the strenuous activity of the evening over (for the moment, anyway) Father Milton felt the chill of the air on his flesh. He wiped what sweat was left from his body with a wool blanket, which he then tossed across the Indian woman's upper half, leaving her naked bottom exposed for his viewing. She had a fleshy flower that protruded between her legs, which he found odd and alluring. Satan's slit came in many tantalizing forms, he'd come to know. He pulled on his long underwear and fastened its buttons all the way to his neck, then donned the black cassock that Barrier Ridge parishioners were accustomed to seeing him in.

Now, Father Milton sat at the small card table that occupied the room, upon which was a bottle of bourbon, a glass, and a Bible. He poured a snort of whiskey and disposed of it quickly, blowing the hot aftertaste out in a satisfying sigh. He looked at the Indian woman and her legs and bottom and folds.

"Do you speak English, child?" he said. She said nothing, of course; all the priest heard was the grunting and moaning of sinful delights in the other rooms. Despite her silence, Father Milton suspected the woman had at least a rudimentary understanding of what he was saying. Had she not reluctantly gone to the bed when he'd told her to do so? And had she not rolled to her stomach when he'd told her to get her tit side on the mattress? She knew more than she was letting on. He poured another drink and down it went.

"Child," he continued, using his most concerned and fatherly voice, "do not hold the sins of lust against me. I am a man of the Lord and am here to help you if I can. To pray for you and feed you and clothe you. Speak your worries to me, child, for when you speak to me, God Himself is listening."

Father Milton doubted the squaw would respond and that was okay; he probably wouldn't understand her broken English anyway. But he enjoyed exposing the vulnerability of others. Inciting both men and women to tell him of their concerns and fears and, most of all, sins was perhaps the most enjoyable part of the priesthood, for him at least. Confessions were the highlight of his week, without a doubt. On more than one occasion, Father Milton was driven to masturbation because of the sinful confessions of his parishioners.

Like when Wendy Gilbert, wife of the mayor,

confessed to sleeping with, not one, but *four* different men in the span of two days—and loving it—Father Milton called off confessions for the rest of the day and retreated to his private quarters behind the church to relieve himself. But it wasn't only confessions of a sexual nature that caused burning in his loins. Clyde Morton confessing to smothering to death his own 79-year-old mother with a pillow had done it. And Lord, the confessions of the sheriff's daughter, Elizabeth Hughes, had caused Father Milton almost as much pleasure as they had nightmares. He wasn't sure how much he could believe from a girl who was crazy enough to eat the devil with horns on, but her confessions were damn entertaining, if nothing else.

It appeared Father Milton would get no such thrill tonight—no confession of deeds done wrong or tales of wounds inflicted upon her or stories of her maddening life on the plains as a savage. But then, the squaw spoke.

"Do you mean it, Father?" Her voice was soft and fearful. And to the priest's surprise, her English was clean, though it wavered slightly as she sobbed.

Father Milton was startled, the bourbon he was in the midst of pouring splashing out of the bottle in greater volume than intended. He quickly drank what he'd poured and wiped the evidence from his lips. "Yes, my child," he said and stood from his chair, walking over to her and kneeling at the bedside. "I'm here for you, child. Speak to me and speak to God." His heart thundered with anticipation. "What is your name, child?" A long moment passed and the priest worried the squaw was having second thoughts.

"Whispering Wind," she said at last, still laying on her side facing the window.

"Whispering Wind," Father Milton echoed, placing a hand on her wool covered shoulder. "A beautiful name. And what have you to say?"

Again, a long pause. Then: "I'm a captive of those men, Father."

The priest squeezed her arm and sighed sympathetically. He'd already suspected this, of course, and didn't much care. A woman—especially an Indian woman—was far less sinful when under the supervision of a man or group of men. "I see," he said. "And have they harmed you, child?" Lord, how he hoped they had and he hoped she would tell of it in great detail.

"At times, yes," she whimpered. "And they . . . they use me without . . . without asking."

"Rape," Father Milton said, nodding, not reflecting on the act he'd so recently completed. "These sound like sinful men, my child. Tell me of them and of their deeds. Tell me and let God wash away your pain and sorrows." His stomach fluttered with anticipation and he felt his tooleywag stiffening.

The squaw rolled towards him, tightening the blanket around her. There were fresh tears in her eyes. "I think they will kill me eventually, Father. They are violent men, except for the one."

"Violent, you say? Tell me, child." This was getting good. If only she would spill the details. Father Milton didn't give one damn about helping the squaw— Whimpering Wind, as he was mentally calling her—but he wanted to hear it all from her quivering lips.

"Yes, they've hurt me. But that's not all, Father. I believe they're . . . bank robbers."

This caused the priest to pause. If there was anything Father Milton adored as much as the Bible and the succulent folds of a woman's honey hole, it was money, and being a man of God was lucrative business in Barrier Ridge. His excitement instantly transformed into urgent concern. The lone bank in town held a substantial cache of money for both himself and the church. "Bank robbers, you say?" the priest said, gripping her arm tight and staring into her dark eyes. "Are you sure?"

"Yes. I'm almost certain."

"What are their names, woman? Tell me!" He said this with frustration, as if the woman was not readily answering his questions. To Father Milton, his money was already in grave danger with them simply being in town.

"I . . . I don't know all of them," she said as fresh tears poured from her eyes.

"Tell me what you know!"

"Tate. The Tate Gang, that's what they call themselves or what the law named them."

"The Tate Gang," Father Milton said. The name sounded vaguely familiar, but it didn't matter. No matter who they were or what their names were, they had the same fate barreling towards them. Standing up now, the priest said, "I'm gonna go pay a visit to the sheriff now, get this all straightened out. Don't you move your little Indian ass from this bed, you hear? You'll be safe here."

"Yes, Father," the squaw said.

An hour later, as a frigid wind howled outside and

A SAVAGE BREED

a former slave turned madam played Beethoven on the saloon's piano, the Tate Gang was taken into custody, along with their squaw.

5

"**My leg is** killing me where that fat Mexican bitch shot me. I think the damn thing is going sour."

Noel, who'd said this, shivered, wrapped in wool and too close to the fire. Crow sat across the dwindling flames from him smoking from Dom's corncob pipe and listening to howls of coyotes and wind. He wondered if a particularly swift wind screeching through the mountains could cause the coyotes to begin their chain of howls. Probably so, he thought. Whispering Wind—an ironic name in such a windy place—was sleeping now, by the looks of it. Her eyes were closed and she no longer trembled; only Crow and Noel were left awake.

"You hear me?" Noel said, his voice scratchy like a saw on wood.

"I did," Crow said. He figured Noel's leg was indeed sour and making him sick. His limp had been getting worse for days and now his flesh had a constant flushed appearance. And men didn't typically shiver that much when they were close enough to the campfire to curl their nose hairs.

"Well, what do you think, Crow?"

"About what?"

"About my goddamn leg! What the hell you think

I'm talking about? You think I'm asking you to look at the goddamn stars and tell me what's out there? Christ, Crow, I don't understand you sometimes. What do you think about my goddamn leg?"

Crow puffed on the pipe and considered this. He didn't much care about Noel or his leg, or any of the other Tates, for that matter. They were business partners, was all, work associates. If he could trade them in at a general store somewhere for a more agreeable bunch of bank robbers, then he would gladly do so. But, so far as Crow knew, general stores kept no such inventory.

"Well, take your time thinking, Crow. I'll die of old age while your wheels turn."

Crow sighed and said, "It's probably sour and a doc should cut the thing off. If not, I imagine you'll die within a week. But most folks die after amputations too, so . . . " He shrugged, leaving it at that.

"Jesus Christ, Crow," Noel said, his eyes like saucers gleaming in the firelight. "Make my fuckin day, why don't ya. Paint me a perty picture and write me a poem while you're at it, you goddamn sidewinder."

Crow couldn't suppress a meager smile. He puffed the last shreds of tobacco, then set the pipe aside and laid over on his own wool blanket, which had the name 'Wallace' stitched into one corner—presumably the name of one of the dead deputies they'd taken the horses and gear from. Crow closed his eyes. The wind was tapering off and so were the screams of coyotes. The only sounds were that of Connor's snoring, Noel's heavy, labored breathing, and the crackling of fire.

"You telling me that goddamn squaw is the last thing I'll ever stick my pecker in?"

If Noel Tate ever said another word before he died, Crow didn't hear it.

6

A *SHOOSH! SOUND* and a sudden gust of rotten air woke Crow from a dream reliving their capture at the Calico Calaboose at the hands of the no-longer-living Sheriff Hughes and his band of merry men.

The wind had stilled, but a cloud of dust, ash, and embers blew around the camp, enveloping him. He breathed it in and coughed it out as his mind slowly crept out of the saloon and came back to the foothills of the Wichita Mountains.

Must have drifted off while Noel bitched about his leg, he thought. He winced as his eyes fluttered open—nothing like a little sleep to bring out the aches and pains of the previous day; his face and backside were both swollen and sore from his multiple falls during their unsuccessful execution.

"What the hell was that?" Dom said, sitting up.

Seemed it had awakened everyone but Connor, who went on snoring, Richard was rising off his back, rubbing grit from his eyes. Whispering Wind still lay on her side, but Crow could see her looking around worriedly. As for Noel—

"Where the hell is Noel?" Richard asked. He looked to Dom who shrugged, then to Crow. "Crow, you seen him?"

"Nope," Crow said, shaking his head. "Not since I laid down." *And he couldn't have got far on that bum leg*, he thought. *Especially in these mountains.*

"Dom, you seen 'im?"

"Don't you think I woulda told your dumb ass already if I knew where he was?" Dom's voice was harsh, but his eyes, to Crow, appeared confused and alarmed.

He knows as well as I do that Noel didn't go for a scenic walk through the hills in his condition, Crow thought.

"Maybe he's just taking a leak," Dom added, without confidence.

"Noel!" Richard yelled, kicking his covers off and standing. He seemed more angry than worried. "Connor, where's Noel?"

Connor continued snoring.

"Crow, you sure you ain't seen him leave?"

"I did not," Crow said. He too rose to his feet, strapping his belt and holster around his waist, figuring that sleep was most likely done for the night.

"Wake up that Irish fuck!" Richard said.

Crow looked to his left where Connor slept, but did nothing to disturb his slumber. The Irishman had been the first of them to find sleep and it was unlikely he had any idea where Noel was.

"He could barely walk by the time we settled down for the night," Dom said, still seated with a perplexed look on his face.

"Squaw—hey squaw!—where is my brother? Where is Noel? Crow, what the devil is that bitch's name?"

"Whispering Wind," he said, and his eyes met

hers. She was scared. Crow's hand rested on the butt of his revolver as he glanced around the camp. The fire had dwindled, but still provided a sufficient glow to see the immediate area. There was no moon and no stars to help him outside the camp's perimeter, and they didn't have a lantern on hand.

"Whispering Wind, you Indian cunt, where is Noel? Huh? What the hell did you do to my brother?"

"She didn't do anything," Dom said, and Crow was glad he did, before he himself said it.

"How the hell do you know? Crow, wake up Connor."

"She's too scared and stupid, Richard. Just calm down. There is an explanation here."

"She's a goddamn savage! She'd knife any one of us given the chance!"

"If she knifed him, where the fuck's he at?"

"What was that sound that woke us and what was with the dust?" Crow interrupted the argument between the two Tate brothers before it got any nastier. "What was that . . . woosh sound?"

"Woosh sound?" Richard said. "I didn't hear no woosh sound."

"He's right," Dom said. "Something woke us all up."

"It was probably this damn savage bitch doing something to Noel! Where is he, you goddamned bottom-feeder?"

"Shut-up, Richard!" Dom yelled. "I hear something."

Crow heard it too. From above them—far above—came the sound of something—or multiple somethings—in flight. To Crow, it sounded like flags whipping in the wind. Or like kites soaring in a particularly gusty sky. He looked skyward, as did the other men, but could see nothing but blackness.

"What the devil is that?" Richard said, his mouth agape as he scanned the abyss.

Something crashed to the ground mere feet behind Crow, with a noise that suggested both breaking and splattering. Instantly, all three men drew their revolvers, Dom joining the other two by getting to his feet. Crow pulled the hammer back as he whirled to face whatever had fallen from the sky. Though the light from the fire was poor and fading further every moment, there was no mistaking what he saw—the mangled, distorted remnants of a person. Instinctively, Crow pointed his gun at the mess, his hand trembling. *What the fuck is going on?* he thought.

"What is that?" both Dom and Richard said at the same time.

Miraculously, Connor was still snoring, oblivious to everything, and Crow now wished he'd done what Richard said and woke him. He looked over his shoulder, seeing that Whispering Wind was now on her knees, staring at him with wet, worried eyes. "It's a body," Crow said to the Tate brothers.

"A body?" they said in tandem again.

"A body," Crow confirmed, turning his attention back to the pile of twisted limbs and gore.

"Who is it?" Dom said. "Go closer and look, Crow. See if that's Noel."

Who the hell else would it be? Crow thought. But then, considering the perplexing soaring sound that continued overhead, he decided he wasn't sure he could guarantee the body was Noel without getting up close and personal. He elected not to question why Dom or Richard weren't going over to get a closer look themselves. Taking two steps forward, he looked quickly up as the noise of whatever was fluttering around in the dark sky seemed to grow closer. Then he looked back down at the body and took one more step, putting him right above it.

What clothing was left was tattered and red with blood. The arms and legs were warped and broken and pointing in odd angles—the left leg was twisted in such a way that the foot was hanging over the body's right shoulder, with a bone jutting out of the ankle jabbing the man's cheek. And as Crow leaned closer, he was certain this distorted man with an ankle bone in his cheek was indeed Noel. He had the same light brown, balding hair and the same mole above his mouth, which hung open and streamed with blood. His neck was gashed open and the tubes and veins protruded, spilling blood. Noel's abdomen, too, had been ripped open, and his intestines and organs hung out. But it was his right thigh—or what was left of it— that truly worried Crow. From Noel's hip to his knee, there was nearly no meat left at all, only threads of pink flesh clinging to the man's femur, as if something had been gnawing on it like a dog does a turkey leg. *Shit*, he thought.

"It's Noel," Crow said, eyeing the skies again.

"What?" Richard said. Crow heard the brothers approaching now.

"I said—"

Swoosh!

It came from behind and to the side of Crow—but

seemed to be everywhere—and the air rippled with a wave of dust and ash. He whipped around, his revolver leading his eyes, just in time to see something disappearing back into the darkness of the sky. It had taken flight from amidst their camp—gone in an instant—and it was dark gray or brown in color, but it was difficult to ascertain in the low light. And, Crow noticed, Connor was no longer sleeping at the side of the fire. He wasn't there at all.

Then Dom and Richard were firing their guns into the sky—*BLAM! BLAM! BLAM!* Each of them fired until their ammo was spent, though Crow searched the skies and couldn't imagine they were seeing anything other than blackness to shoot at. All the same, he now had his gun pointed skyward, ready to fire if he saw the slightest movement. He glanced down, seeing that Whispering Wind had pulled her blanket over her head and curled into a ball, then back at the two remaining Tates staring up with identical looks of horror, trails of smoke rising from the barrels of their guns.

"What was it?" Crow said, and he noticed after the ringing in his ears caused by gunfire dissipated, that he again heard the sound of fluttering movement in the skies. Only now, it was accompanied by screams. Connor—who else could it be?—howled in agony as if from a great distance. There were no words or coherence, only screams. And then the screams stopped. But the fluttering of wings continued.

"It took goddamn Connor!" Richard yelled, reloading his Colt as he did so.

"Took him right off the fuckin ground," Dom said as he, too, reloaded.

"What did? What took Connor?" Crow said, looking skyward again as he asked, suddenly being pelted in the face by droplets of moisture. *Rain?* he thought, but even before he wiped the substance from his cheek and inspected his fingers, he knew what it was: blood.

"Whatever took him is still up there!" yelled Dom. "Don't you hear the bastards? Get to shooting!"

"I'm not firing without a target, goddamnit!" he shouted back. "We don't have unlimited ammunition!"

Just then, something fell into the fire, sending sparks and embers flurrying about them. There, blackening and bubbling amongst the coals and burning wood was a severed arm, the jagged bone above the elbow jutting from the mangled flesh like an ancient tree trunk.

"Son of a whore," Richard said, sounding close to tears. "What in God's name is going—"

Then, something swooped down and snatched Dom in its claws and was airborne again. But before it could disappear into the blackness, Crow unloaded on it.

PART TWO:

THE VENGEFUL

A SAVAGE BREED

1

JAMES HAGGARD HALTED the pony's gallop half a mile from the Comanche camp—where that pack of bloodthirsty savages was going to meet their end this morning—dismounting and tying her to a mesquite tree, then continuing the rest of the way on foot, his rifle cocked and held at the ready, his revolver, too, cocked in its holster. He was ready for blood. But blood had been spilt before he got there.

He approached from the east and saw the tips of three tipis when he crested the first hill, then mounted the next hill and could see them in clear view only a short distance away. Haggard knelt between a large stone and an ancient, twisted oak, peering upon the Indian encampment, teeth grit, sneering. The Comanches had been there only a few months. Haggard reckoned they were waiting for buffalo to move through, or a cattle drive from Texas to be herded through the plains to the east, at which point they could sweep in and steal a substantial number without notice.

You could never tell with Indians. Thieves and drunkards and wagon burners and murderers, the whole lot. Sure, Haggard had known a decent Indian or two (one, he was sure, was a fairy, and the other had been deaf and just didn't take to the rambunctious nature of his comrades), but his days of trying to distinguish between the good and bad ended when he came upon his butchered wife and daughter.

He saw no movement around the tipis. Though it was still morning and the ground still frosty, he found this odd. At the center of the camp was a long-extinguished fire, the coals and fragments of logs black and producing no smoke. The door flap to one of the tipis shuttered nervously in the wind. There were no horses and no men—no signs of life at all.

Suddenly, Haggard was certain they'd heard him coming. He'd galloped the pony too close and they heard him. Before he came upon the settlement, they'd made off on their horses and were circling around to attack him, the sneaky bastards. He looked over his shoulder, his heart pounding against his ribs. Nothing, not a sound but the wind. *And I would have heard them fleeing on horses, wouldn't I?* he thought. But they didn't have to ride off. They could have snuck away on foot, leading their horses, and still be approaching him from cover with guns and bows ready. Or they could be away on a hunt. *Or they could be asleep!* he thought. *Easy pickins for my Winchester!*

Taking a deep breath, Haggard stood and descended the hill.

As he approached the first tipi, walking slowly and silently, he moved aside its door flap with the barrel of his rifle and peered in. There was a blanket and a basket of pecans and some furs, and even a small bow that looked like it was meant for a toddler—a murderer in training, as far as he was concerned—along with a crude doll made of straw, but no occupants. Haggard looked down at the handkerchief doll pinned to his coat and gave it a kiss.

Leaving that tipi, he crossed to another, eyeing the ground and seeing tracks of men and horses that appeared fairly fresh, from the last couple of days, at least. He inspected the dead fire as he passed it, noting frost had accumulated on the coals—a good indication the last time it burned was at least twenty-four hours ago.

He came to the door flap of the second tipi, looking briefly over to the third where the flap continued whipping with the wind, then, turning back to the second and holding the Winchester out, began to open it. The door flap flew open before him and all he saw was deer skin clothing and black hair and rage.

Or fear? a small, almost silent voice whispered in his head. But it was too late to contemplate—he pulled the trigger.

The Winchester roared. The young Comanche – a boy, no more than twelve – pitched backward, clutching at the bloody hole in his chest, eyes wide in a horrified stare. From further inside, a woman screamed.

"Kee!" she screamed again, hovering over the boy, fists covering her mouth. She didn't appear to notice as Haggard chambered another round and leveled the rifle at her head.

He paused for a moment, watching the woman cry, then recalled Sarah and Meredith and what some savage lowlife – that, for all he knew, had been spit out of this woman's pussy – had done to them. He pulled the trigger. Her head exploded, splattering blood and brain across the rear of the tipi.

Haggard backed away, looking at the bodies of the deceased, thinking—regretting? —what he'd done. When he heard movement from behind him, he whirled, but too late. A heavy blow struck the back of his head, then again to his temple. He yelled and swung his rifle wildly, the barrel hitting something and eliciting a holler of agony. Before Haggard, dizzied, his vision cloudy, could discern what he'd hit, he went down. Everything went black.

2

IMAGES CAME TO him like intermittent thunderclaps.

Here was Sarah—lovely Sarah—sitting on the hillside in Little Rock where they'd enjoyed their first picnic together, her blonde hair, much to her irritation, whirling erratically in in the breeze. Eventually, she gave up trying to sweep it out of her face, deciding to tie it up with several long shoots of ryegrass. She smiled and said, "There we go, that's better. Now you can kiss me." Which was exactly what James Haggard did, taking her in his arms, swinging her down the way he'd seen it done in a stage play in downtown Little Rock (his technique was sloppy from lack of practice, but at least they stayed on their feet), and planting his lips on hers. It was their first kiss and they were both sixteen.

Here was Sarah beside him on the wagon as they moved west, just the two of them. She was in her best Sunday dress, despite Haggard telling her that traveling over rocky trails and through creeks and brush might require some britches. She had smiled at him and said, "I reckon if the going gets rough, I'll come out of my dress. But there is no way in hell I'm leaving Arkansas looking anything but my best and with my head held high." She sang almost constantly that first day, sang so much that she could hardly speak the following. She'd loved the adventure of it and didn't mind the hardships; all the way to Barrier Ridge, she never complained.

Here was Meredith, only days old, swaddled in a blanket in Haggard's arms with her curious eyes staring into his. He'd been sitting on a downed tree just south of their cabin, near the edge of their little hill, looking down on the valley that was Barrier Ridge, a gentle and soothing breeze blowing around them. She cooed and Haggard cooed back at her, stroking her cheek with his finger. She felt so delicate. He knew he would love and protect her until the day he died.

Here came a storm, menacing clouds spitting lightning and pouring rain. Sarah and Meredith huddled under the table as the winds howled outside, making the cabin creak like old knees. Haggard peered out the window, fascinated by the power of nature. "Get away from there!" Sarah yelled at him. "That wind and that window are gonna get in an argument, and your face will be the one to pay for it." She was always saying cautious stuff like that. Haggard may have been a hardworking man, and he was loyal and strong and dependable. But he was not what most would call intelligent. Sarah was, however. She could read, for one, but more, she thought critically. She could see the good *and* bad in every situation, and foresaw all the possible outcomes and angles. So, after watching the wind abuse the trees outside his cabin a moment longer, Haggard stepped away from the window and joined his wife and daughter beneath the table. They played cards down there while the storm ran its course.

A SAVAGE BREED

Here he was trying to teach Meredith how to ride her new pony. It was a young, feisty mare, prone to take off and buck and act silly for little reason at all. She wasn't easy to train, and neither was Meredith. "Can I call her Blue Bonnet, Daddy?" she asked as Haggard again lifted her five-year-old frame atop the pony's saddle. "Whatever you like," he said. "Why Blue Bonnet, honey?" Sarah asked, standing alongside the mare, gently brushing her with a curry comb to keep her calm. "Cause I like blue bonnets," Meredith said, smiling and taking hold of the reins. She was relentless. By the end of the day, Meredith had Blue Bonnet under her spell.

Here was Haggard, horseless, staggering home after his unsuccessful hunt. With the cabin in view beneath the moon and clouds, he noticed that no light shone through the windows. Nor was there a lantern hung outside the door, as Sarah would always do when the elements kept him out past sundown. He quickened his pace. Shoving open the door, he called, "Sarah! Meredith! Where are y'all?" Only the wind answered, with its creaking gusts. He pushed aside the table and moved the chairs and called for them louder. Still nothing. The shotgun hung on the wall where it always did, beside the extinguished lantern, which Haggard grabbed and lit. The moment he turned around, the lantern illuminating the cabin's main room, he saw them in the corner, partially hidden behind the rocking chair and stones of the fireplace. He could see their blood-soaked dresses. "No!" he screamed, sprinting to them, seeing dozens of deep lacerations across both their forearms. Defensive wounds, he understood. They had held their arms up to protect themselves from the chopping blows of their murderers. But, eventually, the blows became too painful and their arms fell. And then it was their faces that took the trauma. But it hadn't ended there.

3

HAGGARD'S EYELIDS PEELED apart, and for a moment he didn't have a clue where he was. His head throbbed. He was cold, shivering in a stiff wind. The clouds seemed to be moving abnormally fast. Or maybe he was the one moving. Yes, perhaps he was in the back of a wagon, being carried to the doctor due to some sort of injury. What injury, though? His head? Yes, that must be it—he had been injured and Sarah went for help and now he was being taken to the doctor in Barrier Ridge. Dr. Thorp, Haggard believed his name was. But he didn't feel the jostling typical of a ride in the back of a wagon, nor hear the rickety sounds produced by such travels. All he saw was the movement of the clouds. Or did he? He felt dizzy, nauseated. "Sarah?" he said, weakly.

Simply saying her name brought it all back. His squinting eyes shot wide open. He'd been attacked after shooting those filthy, no-good Indians. He sat up fast, causing his already throbbing head to throb even more. Sprawled in front of him was an elderly Comanche man dressed in buckskin, his arms splayed out to his sides. The man wasn't moving, and, as Haggard struggled to his feet, he noticed the Indian, baggy-browed, hook-nosed son-of-a-bitch, had a bloody gash along his temple, presumably where Haggard hit him with the rifle. *Lucky shot*, he thought. *I never even saw the old bastard.* A fist sized stone lay within reach of the old man—probably what he'd used to clobber Haggard over the head—so he kicked it away.

Haggard reached down—indeed, he *was* dizzy—to retrieve his Winchester, chambered the next round, and pointed it at the Indian's head, right where the old fuck spun his spokes and came up with the idea to chop his family to pieces and—

Just then, the man's eyes fluttered open and went wide when he saw the gun. The elderly man pleaded something in Comanche.

"Nope," Haggard said, shaking his head, "don't talk to me in your savage language. You got about two seconds to make peace with God before I kill you."

"Please," he said in heavily accented English, "don't shoot."

"If you think begging will keep me from shooting you dead, then you're about as sharp as a goddamn cannon ball. I'm killin' you and that's that. But seeing as you speak a little English, you're gonna tell me who killed my family last night. And then, you can tell me where the rest of your savage clan are."

Propping up on his elbows, his leathery, creased face (uglier than an old goat's hindquarters, in Haggard's humble opinion) grimacing as he did so, the old man said, "I know nothing about you, white man. But you just killed my daughter and grandson. So, if you think I give a damn about your family, you're wrong."

"That so?" Haggard said, the rifle still leveled. "So,

you know nothing about the savages that broke into my home yesterday and butchered my wife and daughter?"

"I do not," the old man, the lying, no good cattle thief, said, his face stern.

"Where are the rest of you? I know you got some younger men around here somewhere. Some murderous warriors. They're probably the ones that did it. Where the devil are they?"

The old man shook his head. Through gritted teeth, he said, "No one from this camp touched your family, white man."

"You don't know that!" Haggard roared. "Where are they?"

"They're dead!" the old man yelled back. "All of them are dead!"

"What do you mean they're dead? How?"

"I . . . I will show you, if you like. What's left of them is over the next ridge." The old man pointed to the west with his crooked, lying finger.

Haggard's gaze followed the direction he was pointing, seeing one of the last small hills before the mountains began. It was near a mile away. "Like hell I'm following you, you conniving bastard. You think I'm dumb enough to go marching over a hill and into a band of Comanches? My wife was more cunning than I, but I ain't no chickabiddy."

"Do you really think a band of Comanches would have stayed put while you shot two of their own, white man?"

Haggard considered this, figuring he could kill the old man now and make the walk alone. He found the old man's claim that the rest were dead to be unlikely, especially since there were no horses. And Indians, the whole worthless, treacherous lot of them, were damn good liars. The others were probably on a hunt or looting someone's cabin. Maybe *his* cabin, for all Haggard knew. "Where are your horses?" he said. "You didn't account for them with your lies. I suppose they're dead, too, right?"

The old man sighed. "Some, I believe, yes. Some might have run off. We only had five. and—"

"Horseshit," Haggard said. "Who killed them, then? I didn't hear no gunshots until this morning, and that was south of here."

"It was two nights ago. I will show you. Then you can kill me. Or fight me like a man. Like a warrior."

This brittle, old Comanche was challenging him? "I would like nothing more than to do to you what you and your band of killers did to my family. But you will show me what's over the ridge first, old man. Then we'll get down to business.

The old man said nothing this time, only shaking his head.

"Get to your feet and lead the way," Haggard said. "And what's your name?"

The old man staggered to his feet and said something Haggard couldn't understand, much less pronounce.

"The hell does that mean?" he said.

"Raging Fire," he said.

"Raging Fire?" Haggard sneered. "Your raging days are behind you. Now, lead the way."

The old man, Raging Fire, did as he was told, stumbling on his weak, thin chicken legs, his buckskin garments whipping around his emaciated frame with

72

the wind. Haggard retrieved the hat he lost when he'd been knocked unconscious, then followed with his rifle still raised. He momentarily debated fetching Blue Bonnet, but decided it was unnecessary.

The frost was slowly melting from the ground, though the brisk breeze didn't offer any relief from the cold. The sun apparently was uninterested in peeking through the overcast skies. Haggard kissed the head of the handkerchief doll pinned to his coat, noting the droplets of blood there—Meredith's, no doubt. How scared had she been when those savages attacked her and her mother? Had she known she was going to die, that her life would end promptly at eight years old? How long had she suffered? How long had Sarah suffered? Was Sarah alive when one of those filthy Indians shoved his knife in her crotch?

Their grave—he buried them together—had been dug and Haggard was lifting his wife, preparing to lay her to rest, when he decided they deserved better than being put in the ground in bloodied garments. So, being gentle, as if he might have harmed them, he removed their house dresses, starting with Meredith, crying as he did so, then outfitting her in her favorite blue dress. (It had been her Easter dress that spring.) He then went to Sarah and began removing her house dress, but froze cold when he saw her undergarments. Like her dress, her white undergarments were stained red with still drying blood. But the pantaloons weren't just stained, they were soaked through with crimson between the legs. Haggard silently prayed that it had been nothing more than menstruation. but he knew better. Upon seeing her privates—she'd been knifed there countless times, her womanly parts nothing more than shredded meat—Haggard broke down, wailing and hammering his fist on the ground.

As he and the old man made their way up the ridge, Haggard tried to shove this thought away. But it was stuck with him and wasn't likely to ever leave. His furious, bloodshot eyes stared at the cock-sucking poltroon in front of him, continuing his ascent, however slowly, his thin gray hair blowing like dead grass.

I should just shoot him now, Haggard thought. *Shove the barrel of my Winchester up his scrawny ass and pull the trigger. It wouldn't be justice, but it would be a start. Every Indian—the savage fucks!— every single one I see for the rest of my days is going to die.*

Raging Fire came to a halt at the top of the ridge and Haggard stopped alongside him, thoughts of shooting the old man momentarily forgotten.

"What the hell happened here?"

4

OLD THOUGH HE WAS—and weak and dizzy and in pain from the rifle striking his skull—Raging Fire was still a cunning Comanche and quick when he needed to be.

While the white man stared at the valley below, he felt for the hidden pocket within the seam of his buckskin trousers, making sure the knife—a deadly, razor sharp tool he got in a trade from an Apache over two decades ago—was still there. It was.

"What the hell happened here?" the white man said.

"I will tell you," said Raging Fire, touching the smooth birch handle of the knife. He could have it out in an instant, opening the white man's throat as easily as the belly of a trout.

But first, he would tell his tale. And then he would strike. For his family. His daughters, his grandson. For Fragrant Lily, for Howls At The Moon, and for his poor lost Whispering Wind, he would kill this man.

5

WHISPERING WIND and Morning Sun had been kidnapped five weeks prior by a gang of Mexican bandits as they drove what were likely stolen cattle through the territory. The Comanche men who followed their trail discovered the cattle had been sold on the cheap in Lawton. Stories varied on where the gang went from there. Some townsfolk said north, some said south into Texas, and still others said they fled back west towards Barrier Ridge and the Wichita Mountains. But all the stories had one thing in common: the women remained in tow, captives of the bandits.

The Comanche men had split up to pursue each lead, but whatever route the bandits had taken, the trail had been lost to the elements.

Raging Fire, their elder and unofficial chief, had stayed behind while the other men searched for his daughter and the other girl. Age, and pneumonia the previous winter, had left his health too questionable for such a journey. When all three groups returned to camp long-faced and emptyhanded, with nothing but hungry stomachs, Raging Fire fell to his knees with tears streaming down his creased face, pleading with all the gods of Earth to bring the women home safely.

Divine intervention was needed. He told his band of Comanche brethren they would perform the Eagle Dance that very evening.

Typically, the Eagle Dance was reserved for spring, when eagles were more active in these areas, and thus more inclined to carry messages to the gods on their travels between heaven and earth. But dire circumstances such as these called for such a ceremony.

They performed it in the valley over the ridge, away from their camp. A large fire was built. One of the men donned wings and a war bonnet made of the fallen feathers of eagles and other birds of prey. His face was painted, as were the faces of everyone else. Even Raging Fire, as he sat high on the ridge smoking his pipe and chanting for a commune with the gods, did so with his chiseled face colored red, black, and yellow.

He who wore the wings danced around the high-reaching fire as evening turned to night. The other Comanche—men, women, and children alike—beat on drums and sang to the stars until their throats were as if lined with sand stone. And even then, they kept singing for the return of Whispering Wind and Morning Sun.

Only when the eagle dancer was jerked violently from the ground did the chanting and drumming halt.

He had been replicating the soaring motions of an eagle—arms outstretched, the sheen of feathers reflecting the fire's glow, which raged against the black sky, legs taking him in a slow, smooth zigzag pattern, body dipping and rising the way bird does at the will of the wind—when, like a bolt of lightning, something struck from above.

It enveloped him, and exploded back into the

skies, leaving only a plume of dust and a scatter of feathers floating like autumn leaves to the ground. There one instant, gone the next.

There was a collective gasp. Raging Fire, atop the ridge, rose on shaking legs, his pipe falling from his grasp. For a moment, he thought a mighty eagle had plucked the dancer from the ceremony, intent on delivering him and their message to the gods. He'd never heard of such a thing occurring, even in legends. But it *was* possible.

Then, from the sky, the screams started. And tearing sounds. And sounds of bones being pulverized. And, above it all, the sound of immense, flapping wings

Blood rained down the drummers below. The screaming from above ceased as quickly as it began, but the screaming of women and children commenced, and the men began shouting. Only Raging Fire stood silent, watching with petrified horror and bewilderment.

As if the screams and shouts were the clanging of a dinner bell, more shadows swooped down from the night skies. The things struck fast, faster than any bird of prey ever witnessed by Raging Fire. His old eyes saw little more than blurs silhouetted against the fire as the defenseless Comanche fell under attack. If any among them had brought bows, knives, guns, or other weapons, they hadn't the time to brandish them. Within moments, every single participant of the Eagle Dance but himself had been taken to the skies. Even horses were carried away—Raging Fire saw a horse torn in two as one flying things clutched its head and another its hindquarters.

A SAVAGE BREED

Body parts and blood showered down. Soon, the screams ended and flesh stopped falling from the skies. The flapping of giant wings faded into the distance, then disappeared altogether.

Only then did Raging Fire's legs escape their petrified state and carry him down the ridge and into the valley of dead Comanche.

6

THE SMELL OF decay reached Haggard even from on the top of the ridge. He saw body parts and innards strewn amongst the grass and rocks, and he the charred remnants of a great fire.

"You're telling me," Haggard said gruffly, without taking his eyes off the scene of the massacre, "that some kind of winged creatures just flew upon your little band of savages and killed every goddamn one of you? You expect me to believe that?"

"I am only telling you what happened."

Although the old man did seemed to be telling some version of the truth, Haggard supposed it didn't matter much anymore. Blood had spilled on both sides and there would be a reckoning. But damned if it wasn't a peculiar story the old bastard spun.

"That's all pretty hard for me to swallow. And what about that boy and that squaw I just shot, huh? You said those things from the sky killed everyone but you."

The old man went solemn. "Howls at the Moon and Fragrant Lily had fallen ill. I told them to stay in the tipi, keep warm and drink tea. I thought they were safe. But you killed them, you evil white devil!"

With this last proclamation, the sneaky fuck

lashed out, brandishing a blade from Haggard knew not where. It swept in an arcing, violent stroke meant to open Haggard's throat. Raging Fire was fast for a withering old man draped in sagging Indian flesh, his eyes sunken into his skull wide with fury, his teeth (of which few he had) gritted as his lips sneered back to reveal blackened, diseased gums, but he wasn't fast or mean enough.

Haggard lurched backwards, dipping his head as he did so. The knife that was meant for his neck sliced open his chin instead. Then the rifle was coming around, colliding with Raging Fire's arms, snapping bones like dry twigs, and knocking the knife from his grasp. The old man lost his balance, stumbling, then regaining his feet. He stared at Haggard with abject horror, mouth agape and eyes like saucers. The hopeless heathen looked as if he were going to say something—perhaps a conceit to Haggard's victory or a farewell to whatever family lived on, or maybe to beseech the gods to allow him passage to the afterlife—but whatever it was, it went forever unsaid.

With one report of Haggard's Winchester, Raging Fire hit the dirt.

7

IT WAS NIGHTFALL before Haggard reached the spot where he'd left Blue Bonnet, and his dead daughter's pony was no longer there.

Stolen by Indians, no doubt, Haggard thought, *the thieving sons-of-bitches*. He sat on a stone and mulled his options, eventually dozing into nightmares of Sarah and Meredith's bloodied bodies clawing themselves from their shallow graves and pleading for him to breathe life back into them.

Gunfire woke him when the moon was high behind cloudy skies, his neck sore from the odd posture of his slumber. Listening to the barrage of shooting to the north and west of him, he sighed and rose to his feet and grasped his rifle, loading three rounds to replace the three he used that day, and took to walking in that direction. It ceased not long after, but he kept going.

At some point, during those dark hours, he came once more upon Raging Fire, and saw something gleaming beside the old crooked Comanche's lifeless body as the clouds parted just briefly around the moon's glow. It was the knife. Haggard retrieved it from the grass, examined his own dried blood on the blade and a strange etching of four connected spirals on the handle, then tucked it into his coat pocket. He wondered if it was the knife that had been used to kill his family. Then he walked on.

PART THREE:

THE GIRL

1

"IT CERTAINLY IS a tragedy, Mrs. Hughes," Father Milton said, taking her recently-widowed hands in his and squeezing them tight. "Of that, you are correct." He held a look of sorrow and devastation on his face, and was even able to bring his eyes to the brink of tears, giving them that glossy, watery look of despair. It was a gift.

The Hughes house was still cold in the mid-morning, so Father Milton briefly relinquished his grip to toss a couple of logs in the fire place and stoke the flames. He brushed his own hands clean and returned to Mrs. Hughes, again taking and petting hers. They were soft, smooth—not calloused or overly dry like those of women of the plains often were. He wondered how she kept them so, and wondered how they would feel on his body.

"I just don't know how I can manage, Father," Mrs. Hughes sobbed. "Rutherford was my world! I cooked for him and cleaned for him and washed his clothes. I told him, Father! I told him to give up being the sheriff. I told him that Satan has demons walking all over this earth and they would like nothing more than to take down a man of the law. I warned him, Father!"

"Indeed, child, I've no doubt you did," he said, removing one hand from hers and caressing her hair, stroking it from her forehead down to the nape of her neck. He tried to make eye contact, but she was staring at her lap. He wanted to see her tears and pain and sorrow and fears. Mrs. Hughes wasn't giving *all* the goods just yet, but she would; Father Milton was patient. Then, perhaps, she would give a little more; weak women were known to react strangely in times of grief. "And you are correct, of course, that demons walk amongst us looking for men of power to place in the dirt. Child, you wouldn't believe the evils I've encountered and endured as a man of the cloth. Sometimes it's . . . it's more than I can bear. The evils of this world take a toll on my body, if I'm being quite honest. Sometimes, it's only the touch of a woman that soothes me, driving the pains of my ongoing struggle with Satan right from my flesh. Did you know—"

At this point, that Father Milton looked back at her, having let his gaze wander as he told her of his everlasting strife with malevolent denizens of Hell, and she was, what, staring blankly at her damned knee? Even her tears seemed to have abated for the time being. This was not what the priest wanted. It was, in fact, quite unacceptable given the situation, with the sheriff's fat corpse being loaded up by the undertaker just outside. Perhaps a change of tactics was in order. He had moved a little too quickly, that's all. He, Father Roger Milton III, would bring this woman back to the grief-stricken world where she was currently supposed to reside.

"Child," he said tenderly, squeezing her hand, "if

I might inquire, what was the last thing you and Mr. Hughes did together? You see, the Lord says we should embrace the memory of our lost loves. So, if you don't mind . . . "

"What?" Mrs. Hughes said, barely audible, her eyes blinking and finally coming into focus. "What's that, Father? I'm sorry, I—"

"I said, what was the last thing you and Mr. Hughes did together?" Father Milton repeated, and although he was growing irritated, he kept any sign of it from his voice.

"Oh," she said timidly, looking about herself as if she suddenly wasn't sure where she was. At last, she said, "We ate breakfast together, over yonder at the table, this very morning before the sun came up."

"Ate breakfast, you say? Well, that's a wonderful memory. Tell me a little more about it, so as the memory doesn't fade and disappear like a splash of water on the dirt." She no longer looked upset and this worried him. Not a hint of tears. But he would get them; he was good at what he did. "Tell me about this breakfast, child."

"Rutherford," she started, staring (blankly, again) out the small window of the main room, "Rutherford said the eggs were overcooked and I shouldn't have made Elizabeth get up so early to bake the bread."

"Uh, perhaps we should think of another—"

"He said I was lazy and couldn't cook and that my crocheting was too loose and everything I made unraveled within a month."

"Perhaps we should think back on another memory, Mrs. Hughes," Father Milton said. "One you're more fond of, you know."

"He said as bad a cook as I am, he didn't understand how I kept myself as plump as a musk ox at full gestation."

Father Milton sighed and put his head in his hands. This was going poorly, indeed. Whatever excitement had developed over the course of the hour since he'd first arrived was gone. If he were to have any chance of making this a worthwhile visit to the Hughes house, he would need to think of something quick, and preferably without bringing up that girl.

"Father?"

"Yes, child," he said, struggling to maintain the concern in his voice. He raised his head, noticing she was looking at him, straight into his eyes. "Yes, child?"

"Elizabeth is gone, and I know not where." She grabbed his hands again. "To the west, I think."

Father Milton nodded sympathetically. "The west is . . . dangerous. It's best if we not—"

"There are demons, evil things, that way, Father."

"Demons all over, my child."

"I need you to go fetch her, Father, before the demons take her. I know she's not *right*, but perhaps with prayer, maybe even an exorcism, we can help her. I need you to fetch her, please, Father!"

Father Milton sat stunned, his mouth agape, his hands no longer holding hers, simply being held. This day had spiraled south in a hurry. Why had he decided to visit Mrs. Hughes first, for God's sake? There were several other families that had lost loved ones this day. He proceeded to tell her as much: "Mrs. Hughes, surely you must know I have other families to visit. The sheriff was not the only man to—"

A SAVAGE BREED

"This is an emergency, Father! Elizabeth needs us! She needs God!"

"Needs God?" he echoed, utterly annoyed now. "You think God can help her?"

"I'll pay you! I'll give you everything we have!"

Ten minutes later, as Father Milton opened the door to leave while shoving a bundle of money wrapped in paper and twine deep in his coat pocket, he turned to Mrs. Hughes and said, "Satan has a lot of demons at his disposal—women and Indians and bandits—but that little girl . . . Lord Jesus, when we get back, you're gonna have to do something about *her*, or I will."

2

"**I THINK MAYBE** I should go by Liz from now on, what do you think? Or maybe Lizzy? Lizzy sounds good. I never have liked 'Elizabeth' a whole hell of a lot, especially the way mother would say it—not that I should be concerned about that any longer. 'Eliiiiiizabeth!' is how she would say it, the old fat hog. Or maybe I should go by Beth. You know, cause that's the last four letters of Elizabeth. You sure don't help much in decision making, you know it?"

It was Lightning, the majestic Andalusian horse formerly ridden by her father, that Elizabeth Hughes spoke to as she rode westward at a leisurely pace. She and the horse were passing through the prairies just south of Barrier Ridge and the mountains were still a good distance ahead. She saw, several hundred yards away, where the captured bandits had gunned down the lawmen, including her father, earlier that morning. The other bodies, it appeared, were still there, but with a gathering of townsfolk around them, so Elizabeth elected to keep her distance. Townsfolk tended not to be very fond of her, especially after she sawed off the hooves of that pony outside the general store. But the damn thing kept getting away from its owner (he was a useless drunkard of a store owner) and running over to the Hughes's property and eating up all the apples off their apple tree. What the hell was she supposed to do?

"Anyway, Elizabeth is more of a lady's name. I ain't interested in being no lady. I'm an adventurer, on my way west to find gold and chinks, whatever that means. Hell, Lightning, I'm like Lewis and Clark or Daniel Boone. Or Tom Sawyer, for that matter. Liz Sawyer, that's me! Or do you think Lizzy or Beth? Lizzy may sound too much like a child's name. What do you think, Lightning? Every time I hear a name with a 'y' on the end, I think of it as childish. Like Davy Crockett! Why in the name of Texas would he go by Davy instead of David or Dave? Or, hell, just go by Crockett. You ever heard of anyone else named Crockett? Not me. Crockett—wildman of the west! Sounds like a pretty good idea to me. But what do I know, I'm just a kid and he's dead, just like Papa. Dead with a hole in his head.

"That was pretty damn smart of you to come back to the stables with Papa dead on your back, Lightning. I reckon you're pretty smart for a horse. You could've told him to pull his gun, however. Or you could've dodged them bullets. Ain't horses supposed to be fast? Maybe not as fast as bullets, I reckon. All the same, that was pretty good of you to come back to the stables. Well done, Lightning!

"Damn, those mountains look pretty far off, don't they? Can't be that far, though. I heard Papa telling Deputy Smith that it was only a day's ride to the western mountains. I reckon we're going pretty slow but that's alright by me. I ain't in no hurry. And it ain't too cold. I wonder how far it is to California. Like, once we cross over them mountains, are we there? I think I heard Papa say there's more mountains west of here. Big ones, I think he said. But these here Wichita Mountains look big enough. If I hadn't got booted from school for strangling that rotten Ms. Finch—she deserved it, believe me—I might know this stuff. I should of brought a map. I bet Papa had a map somewhere at home. I reckon I could find a map in town, too. But I think I'll keep my distance from Barrier Ridge, hence forth. Nothing but a bunch of supposed God-fearing folks who hate children there. They especially hate harmless little girls like me, I've come to find out. Hell, I ain't been fifteen two weeks now—no adult, for sure!—and small, at that. Momma says I was born early and was always small, but that I came out stronger willed than was rightly good for me.

"You know what?" Elizabeth said, bringing the horse to a halt and looking behind her at the meager bag of supplies strapped to the saddle. "We didn't bring no water. And only a loaf of bread to eat. I've got a lot to learn about being an adventurer and explorer, I guess. I reckon I can shoot something to eat. There's all kinds of varmints and coyotes and deer running about. I'm not the greatest shot in Indian country, but Papa taught me alright, I suppose. He lined up some tin cans for me to shoot just outside of town and showed me how to hold the rifle and how to aim it and how to hold my breath when I pulled the trigger. I was plumb impressed at how well I did, Lightning. Papa, though, he got right angry when I shot the head off Mr. Johnson's rooster. Personally, I thought it was a great shot.

"Anyhow, I reckon we'll find something to eat. Finding water, though, that may be a hassle. Ain't there a ravine just a little to the northwest of here? Seems like Papa took me fishing that aways when I was just a little girl. I could always ride back to the house and fetch some water from the well." She turned, looking back the way they'd come. The house was nowhere in sight; even Barrier Ridge was but a speck in the distance.

"Well goddamn, Lightning," she said, slapping the horse's neck hard enough to make it flinch, "we're making some miles, ain't we? Traveled halfway across the valley, anyhow. Hell, at this rate, we may make California in two or three days, wouldn't you say? I sure wish horses could talk. It'll get a bit irritating holding up a one-sided conversation all the way across the west. I bet in the future horses will talk. I bet all animals will be talking in the future, if you ask me. Papa said some scientific folks said people grew out of monkeys and started talking, so why can't horses and cows and giant desert centipedes grow into talking too? That ol' undertaker, Walter—I like visiting him on occasion, when he has some dead folks stacked up—told me that negroes didn't know how to talk 'til they come over here and learned. So, there you go. Horses will learn one day.

"I'm just a rambling like ol' Grandma Hughes used to do, before she had that unfortunate slip off the front porch. And no, I had nothing to do with that . . . well, hell, I guess it don't matter much now. I pushed the old hag. Don't snort at me, Lightning! She was being extremely rude to me, I must say, calling me devil child and rotten and no good. What was I supposed to do? Anyhow, I didn't know she would break her neck—just kinda lucked out with that part.

"Well, we best find that ravine. Then we'll find us a spot to settle down for the evening. Sound good, Lighting, you ol' bitch? You ever been poked by a male horse? They sure have some long peckers."

She rode a little faster then, letting the wind, cold as it was, rush around. It felt refreshing, even as it turned her nose and cheeks cold and made her lungs burn with every deep breath. Elizabeth Hughes felt free. It was the cold air or the expansive prairie or the oncoming mountains that felt refreshing; it was the freedom. But maybe it was all that stuff too. And maybe it was her adventures to come in California. Everything rolled together. She thought perhaps this was the best day of her life, even with Papa getting his face blown off. A far cry from the day Mamma caught Elizabeth putting a frog up her flower—all that was showing was the thing's little brown legs sticking out of her, jerking all around. Was a wonder Momma hadn't keeled over the moment she interrupted the situation. It had felt good until Momma walked in, then the day went sour quick. And this day was a hell of a lot better than the time Elizabeth thought it would be a good idea to go dig up the grave of Opel Williamson and start trying on all the fancy jewelry she was buried with. How was she supposed to know that there was such things as desecration of a grave and grave robbing and necrophilia? She was just a little girl.

The sun was making its descent when, at last, Elizabeth and Lightning reached a shallow creek. It cut jaggedly through the prairie, with trees overhanging it here and there. Beyond the creek—less than a mile, Elizabeth guessed—were the first few foothills of the Wichita Mountains. She figured she could make it by sundown, but what was the rush? After letting Lightning have a long drink of water, and getting a few handfuls for herself, Elizabeth led them up the other side of the creek and tied the horse to a tree there.

"I reckon this spot will do for the night, don't you, Lightning?" she said as she removed the saddle and her belongings from the horse. "I wonder if this ravine has any frogs."

3

A FRONTIERSMAN, Father Milton was not. Not that one needed to be a frontiersman to navigate the prairieland around Barrier Ridge or even the low and relatively unobtrusive Wichita Mountains. But Father Milton preferred to stay within the confines of his hometown, and within reach of his comforts—the church and the bank and the saloons and the whores. That being said, every man had a price that would propel his ordinarily stoic legs to step outside their comfort zone. Three hundred dollars in paper money and a leather handbag of various coins was apparently his.

Still, riding his less-than-fair steed through the blustery winds of Indian Territory as the sun descended before him (it was becoming quite the nuisance for his eyes, despite the overcast skies), he reckoned it probably wasn't enough. His stomach grumbled and he cursed himself for not thinking to bring more than the three apples Mrs. Hughes sent him with, all of which he'd already eaten. Sure, he could have popped into Mac's General Store and picked up some food and supplies, but that would have put him even further behind the little—that wretched thing, Elizabeth Hughes.

A SAVAGE BREED

In all honestly, Father Milton had no desire to find the little trouble-making bitch. If there ever was a thorn in the side of Barrier Ridge's populace, it was none other than Elizabeth Hughes. It was not unusual to come upon her stealing fruit from folks' gardens or throwing rocks at windows just for the hell of it or frying every bug in a ten-mile radius with a magnifying glass—she'd burnt down half of the town's only barber shop doing just that. And the girl had done much worse, Father Milton was well aware. If half the filth she spewed during confession was true—never mind that the good priest quite enjoyed those sessions—then the girl was crazier than a headless cock.

And Mrs. Hughes thought Father Milton and God Himself could help this child? That was even less likely to happen than him, an overweight man of the cloth with no tracking skills whatsoever, finding Elizabeth before a band of Comanche or, worse, the Tate Gang fell upon her and had their way with her. (Not that he'd mind bearing witness to such events, but it was unlikely he could do so in relative safety.) Elizabeth Hughes, whether he found her or not, was what Father Milton considered a lost cause. There was no helping her. He couldn't do it and neither could a thousand *Our Fathers* and a thousand more *Hail Marys*. The priest doubted if God Himself—Praise the good Lord!—could descend on Barrier Ridge and make that little girl into a decent and proper lady. A lost cause, that's what she was. Possibly even a demon wrapped in little girl's flesh. Father Milton wasn't as knowledgeable on demons as he proclaimed, so likely wouldn't wager much money on Elizabeth Hughes being one, but if there was a person on God's earth that was destined for the pits of Hell, it was her.

So, now that Sheriff Rutherford Hughes was getting measured for his final suit courtesy of Walter Dreary, Father Milton wasn't exactly burning up the trails to find his girl. The days of Rutherford protecting his little trouble-making child were as long gone as taxes to the British Crown. While the priest certainly wouldn't mind seeing Elizabeth swinging from the gallows when the townsfolk got hold of her, he wasn't inclined to see what kind of trouble she could cause before that happened. So, he would ride around and see what he could see, sure. For taking the payment, he owed Mrs. Hughes that much. But he wouldn't find her. And even if he did, he wasn't bringing her in. She could ride on to the Rockies or—where was it she was going?—California.

"California," Father Milton chuckled, pulling on his bison fur coat as he rode westward, the sun merely a flicker of light beyond the crests of the mountains. "Lord God, if that girl makes it to California, You can strike me dead. I imagine a sewer rat in New York has a better chance of getting there than she does."

He considered this a moment. He was right, of course, but what if Elizabeth Hughes came to the realization that she couldn't make it to California? What if she decided that her trip west was just a bit too much trouble? What if she decided this when she was still reasonably close, and thus decided to mosey on back to Barrier Ridge?

"Heaven forbid it," Father Milton said under his breath.

A SAVAGE BREED

This was indeed a possibility, he suddenly realized. Perhaps even now she was on the trail back home. For all he knew, he'd passed her in the failing light and she was now closer to Barrier Ridge than he. She could have the whole town burnt down in the time it took him to get back. An exaggeration, of course, but he was worried all the same. He could not let that girl come back to Barrier Ridge. This was his chance—the town's chance!—to get rid of her forever. So, maybe it *was* his duty to find her. Not for Mrs. Hughes and certainly not to bring her home, but for the townsfolk of Barrier Ridge. For his parishioners, for God's country. Yes! For the betterment of God's country, he *had* to prevent this girl's return. But what did that mean, if he happened upon her? Slipping her some money and sending her on her way, pointing her in the direction of the nearest train? Harming her? *Killing her?*

"Whatever it takes," Father Milton said aloud. "Whatever it takes."

First, he needed to find some flat ground to bed down for the night, and some damn food wouldn't hurt. His stomach grumbled again. He would give damn near anything to have a deer or, better yet, a hog cross his path so he could knock it down for some easy dinner. The only firearm he carried was a Colt Army, but at close range it should do the trick. And any kind of meat would do the trick right about now.

As the sun finally blinked out completely beyond the peaks, Father Milton saw a flicker of light—it was flames, likely from a campfire. Judging distance, especially at night, was not one of his strengths, but he imagined the fire was less than a mile away. Not far at all on horseback. And surely whoever was camped out on the prairieland just a few miles outside of town would have something to eat. Thus, he turned his horse in that direction and nudged it with his boot and gave it a gentle rap with the reins, boosting its speed to a fast trot, but not a full gallop. (Going too fast would likely spook whoever was camped around the fire, which could easily result in having guns being pointed at him upon his arrival.)

The cold stung his cheeks as the horse carried him towards the fire, his large belly jostling and grumbling. He'd never been so hungry. He imagined the carcass of a deer or elk or hog or . . . anything—even a coyote—roasting over that fire. He imagined men sitting around, warming their hands by the flames, picking off chunks of meat and throwing them down their gullets, laughing and joking about this and that, telling tales—greatly exaggerated—of their adventures and travels. Maybe they would have a pot of beans going too, or rice or corn. Hell, if the good priest was really lucky, they might have a bottle of whiskey or two, and wouldn't mind sharing with a man who could teach them the ways of the Lord.

Father Milton's eyesight wasn't the best, but as his horse carried him closer he saw that there wasn't a gathering of individuals, only one, unless perhaps others were just not around the fire at the moment. But he saw only one horse, as well, which appeared to be either white or gray. This was fine by him. Maybe even better. One man alone on the frontier was likely to be lonely and want for conversation. Likely he would have no reservations about sharing nourishment and libations with a stranger in exchange for friendly dialogue.

These were the thoughts running through Father Milton's mind when the ground disappeared beneath him. He felt a split second of complete weightlessness as his feet left the stirrups and the horse fell away, as if perhaps he would float the last sixty feet or so to the camp—perhaps, in fact, God Himself had lifted him from the horse and was delivering him to his destination—then downward he fell and everything went black.

4

"WHAT THE DEVIL? Father Milton, is that you down there? What in Christ's name are you doing way out here? Why ain't you tending to your church and your congregation and your whores? Ain't it roundabout whore-o'clock in Barrier Ridge? Usually is at sundown."

Elizabeth Hughes stood at the edge of the creek with her Papa's Henry rifle in her hands. She had the hammer pulled to the rear and the barrel pointed roughly in the direction of Father Milton, though not exactly aiming it at him. She'd heard the horse coming her way and been overcome with anxiety, thinking the gang of bandits that killed Papa had discovered her presence and were coming to do God knows what to her. Then she realized it was only one horse she was hearing and her mind eased a hair, but she grabbed the Henry and actioned the lever, all the same—better safe than sorry! Then she heard it go right over the side without slowing down a damn bit. She heard the horse scream out and heard man holler and then heard them both crash to the bottom—and seeing as the water wasn't but a couple of inches deep at its deepest, she reckoned that drop was a painful one.

"I said, Father Milton, is that your fat ass at the

bottom of this here ravine? Or are my eyes deceiving me and it's actually Walt Whitman down there come to charm me with words?"

"It's me," said a weak, wavering voice that ended in a sob.

"Me who? Mr. Whitman? I sure do like your poems. Get your ass up here and serenade me!"

"It's Father Milton," the voice said.

"Oh," Elizabeth said. She knew as much, of course, but had to play with the priest who'd lost his way. "Well, that's downright disappointing, Father. No disrespect to you, don't get me wrong; you can sling them words pretty good too, enough to have them whores and tramps fawning over you at the Calico Calaboose, anyway. But you ain't no Walt Whitman."

"Help me out of here," the priest said. He rolled over on his back, his bald head pointing towards Elizabeth, and reached up an arm. This was a ridiculous effort, in Elizabeth's opinion; his hand was still a good ten feet away from the toes of her boots at the edge of the creek. She couldn't very well bend down and yank his lard ass up.

"I think your horse broke its neck," she said, looking past the priest to where the horse lay unmoving with its head at an odd angle.

Father Milton, seeming to suddenly remember how he got where he was, also looked, and muttered, "I think so, too." Then, looking back at Elizabeth, he repeated "Can you help me out of here, please?"

"Was that a boy horse?" Elizabeth said.

"What . . . yes, but—"

"Well, goddamn. I woulda let Lightning have a little poke before we headed off into the mountains tomorrow. That was pretty dumb of you to run your horse right off the edge of a ravine, Father. Why didn't God swoop down and carry your fat ass across, and pat you on the bottom and lick your balls and such? And if that was too much trouble, why didn't He at least inform you there was a ravine in your path and you was about to go from riding a horse to swimming in the mud?"

"Please, Elizabeth, reach that gun you're holding over the side and let me pull myself up."

His request to grasp her rifle made Elizabeth think, just what exactly was Father Milton doing out here? He had no business this far west of Barrier Ridge. Hell, he had no business outside of town, at all. She could only think of two reasons he would have ventured this direction. Either he was after those bandits that killed Papa and his deputies (she found this highly unlikely, given the priest's less than courageous personality), or he was after her.

"No," she said. "You can drag yourself out of there, I reckon. And my name ain't Elizabeth no more; it's Liz Sawyer. So, get it right."

"Elizabeth, please! I think my leg may be broken!" Father Milton yelled, almost frantically.

"It's Liz Sawyer. And what in the name of the Holy Ghost do you think I'm gonna do with a broke leg? I'm no doctor, I hate to tell you, I'm just a girl. So, you can pull on your big boy trousers and pull your own self out, or you can pray to the Lord to lift you out or whatever. But I ain't helping. I'll be sitting here by the fire, where it's nice and warm and dry, waiting on you."

So, Liz Sawyer did just that, walking lazily back to the log she'd been sitting on when she first heard the galloping horse (she had pulled three logs and a large rock around all sides of the fire, as if she was expecting company), then plopping down on it and warming the soles of her boots by the flames, making sure to keep the Henry pointed at the area where she expected Father Milton to make his ascent. She heard him grunting and cursing as he moved about, then heard some loose soil give way and heard him slide (or fall) back into the creek. He cursed again—not very proper for a religious man!—and grunted some more as he climbed. The grunting reminded Liz of the sounds her late Papa made when he was fornicating with Momma. Their room was right next to hers and, seeing as Liz, formerly Elizabeth Hughes, never was too fond of sleeping, she tended to hear it every time they were "having relations," as Papa called it. Momma never seemed to make a peep.

Eventually, after a considerable amount of time had passed and a considerable amount of soil was displaced from the bank of the ravine and an even greater amount of curses were spewed, the priest's hands came over the top and he pulled himself out of his temporary dungeon.

"Well done, Father!" Liz Sawyer said. "I'm damned impressed with your resolve. And without the help of God-Almighty, no less."

The priest struggled to his feet, then fell to his knees, breathing hard and wheezing, a thick glob of bloody spittle stretching from his bottom lip to the dirt. Liz noticed his right eye was red where blood vessels must have burst. And there was more blood dripping from his right ear. Between wheezing breaths, he said, "I think I broke some ribs, too."

"Not surprised," Liz said, sticking her pinky in her ear and wiggling it around, then taking it out and plunging it in her mouth and sucking on it. She did this while keeping the other hand on the Henry, which still pointed at the priest, who was now crawling towards the fire. He got slowly to his knees again, wavering ever so slightly, as if a brisk wind might blow him right over, then slid onto one the logs Liz had drug over, directly across from her.

"You have any water?" he blurted and spit a bubbling dollop of blood between his feet.

"Water?" Liz said, sounding astonished. "You just came out of the goddamn creek! You didn't drink none while you was down there?"

"Water?" he said again.

"I ain't got no water, Father Milton. When I get thirsty, you know what I do? I walk right over yonder," she pointed upstream about fifty feet, "where the bank washes away and bend down and get me a couple a handfuls of water, that's what I do. Hell, if you'd had any sense at all you would've just came out over there instead of trying to climb up the bank, like you're some priest turned mountaineer. I'm surprised God didn't point you in that direction, now that I think about it. But I guess He wants folks to do for themselves, huh? That's what Momma always said, anyway. You would know better than me, you're the priest. I'm just a girl."

Father Milton sighed, shaking his head. He stared at the dirt for several minutes, then said, "I'm . . . hungry."

"I'm hungry too. Real hungry."

"You don't have . . . food either?"

"Nope. I reckon you didn't bring any with you?"

He sighed again, shaking his head. Then: "My horse . . . my dead horse. We can . . . we can eat it." His voice was becoming raspy and Liz saw more blood dripping out of the corner of his mouth.

"I ain't eatin' a horse! What kind of savage do you think I am?"

Father Milton shook his head again, spitting blood, sighing and coughing. Liz Sawyer stood up on the other side of the fire, getting a better look at him, and shot him in the chest.

5

IT WASN'T AS if she planned it. Father Milton was practically asking to be shot, with all his spitting blood and whining and complaining and asking for this and that, as if Liz brought Mac's General Store along for her adventures west. And what was he doing out here, anyhow? That was the *real* question.

"Nothing good, that's for damn sure," Liz Sawyer said, still standing with the fire between her and the priest—who was now slumped over on his side with a trickle of blood exiting the hole in his chest. "You weren't out here looking for Jesus, were you? If you were, I reckon I'm sorry. But it's too late now. That was a good shot though, wasn't it? Right where I was aiming! Right in the heart probably, if you got one. How come God didn't stop the bullet from hitting you, I wonder? I mean, if there was ever a time for God to intervene on your behalf, that was it. And, to tell you the truth, as I was squeezing that trigger, I was kinda wondering if lightning—not you, Lightning, you're a good girl!—if lightning was gonna strike me down before I got the shot off. But it didn't. Maybe you ain't such a good priest. Maybe God don't look down on you with quite the gleaming eyes and wide smile you think He does. But what do I know, I'm just a little girl."

A SAVAGE BREED

She laid the rifle on the log beside and walked to Lightning, who was tethered to a large tree over by where Liz intended to sleep when the time came. She brushed the horse's hair with her fingers and kissed her on the nose, then fed her the last few pieces of bread from her pocket. Against the tree, Liz had leaned the saddle and satchel after tying off Lightning. Now, she reached in the satchel and brought out the Bowie knife and unsheathed it. It was heavy in her hand and the fire gleamed off its polished steel. The handle was smooth and fit comfortably in her grip. When she'd turned fourteen, Liz (then known as Elizabeth Hughes) wanted a gun for herself—a Colt revolver, to be exact. Momma, predictably, refused. But Papa had compromised, hiring the best blacksmith in the Territory to fashion her a knife that would last a lifetime. It was a beautiful sight and handy tool, sharp enough to shave with. As Papa had told her on the day she received it, she could use it to hunt, fillet fish, to defend herself, or . . . to cut meat.

Liz went to where Father Milton lay lifeless and sat beside him. Putting the tip of the knife to the pointer finger of her left hand, she twirled it in her right. She liked the way the firelight reflected off of it, slinging shards of light across the ground, the tree, and Lightning. She stopped it twirling and examined the blade again, then shrugged and grabbed hold of the priest's leg by the trousers and yanked. He was heavy; even his leg. Then she brought the Bowie knife down, chopping into the kneecap. This first blow went nearly a quarter of the way through the priest's leg.

"Hot damn, this is a hell of a knife," Liz said,

pulling it free of the knee and inspecting the blade's bloody edge once more. "You see that, Lightning?" she said, looking over her shoulder at the horse. "Went almost halfway through his cotton-pickin' leg in one swoop. I reckon him being mostly fat and not too muscly helps, but watch me get through this bone. I wonder if I should have started at the thigh instead of the knee. I ain't sure which one is harder to cut through."

She pondered pulling his trousers off, but decided that would be a bit too much work on such a large fella. Once she cut through the knee, the pant leg below would slide right off, easy-peasy. She chopped again and blood and flesh splattered around the wound, and Liz felt the crack of bone. Again, she brought the knife down and it cracked into his leg, and she could feel the knee joint flex inward as the bones were pulverized. The knife was stuck this time—stuck in Father Milton's knee! "Give it here, Father. You ain't got no use for my knife." Holding the hilt tight, she jerked it from his leg, flinging scraps of flesh and bone flying. One flap of skin landed in her hair and dangled in front of her eyes. Picking it out and looking at it curiously, she tossed it in the fire.

Grabbing hold of his boot, still muddy from his tumble into the creek, she steadied his leg to keep it from flopping around like a fish as she gave it four quick, hard whacks. The last blow broke through the knee and severed the meat behind it.

"Hell, yes, Lightning! We have ourselves a leg," Liz said, sticking the knife in the dirt and holding up Father Milton's lower leg to show the horse. "Well, it's part of a leg, anyway. Still a leg." She pulled the boot off and tossed it in the fire along with a wet, grimy sock, then she slid off his pant leg. "Oh no. This won't do, Lightning. Look how hairy his goddamn leg his. Look at it! You would think he's half monkey or something. This won't do at all, this ugly fat leg."

She tossed the leg in the fire.

"Dismembering people is a lot of work, Lightning. I wish horses had hands. I bet you could chop through ol' Father Milton in one swipe. Can you believe he wanted to eat his horse? I mean, who the devil eats a horse? Horses are for riding and loving, not eating. What kind of God-fearing man wants to eat a horse? I wouldn't eat no horse, Lightning, so don't you worry. I would starve my little self to death before I'd eat you. I do wish you had some hands, though. For one thing, you could straighten Father Milton up so he wouldn't be laying all awkward, making it hard for me to chop on him. For another, you could probably chop him to bits in no time. I gotta find a spot without hair."

Liz went about removing the priest's clothing. The one remaining boot on his one remaining foot was the easy part—she tossed it in the fire too. But because of Father Milton's substantial girth, the rest of his outfit was another story. After some fruitless yanking and pulling, she retrieved the knife and sliced up his trousers, cassock, and fur coat in a matter of minutes, and went about pulling away the tattered remains.

"Mercy, Father," Liz said, wiping her brow when she at last had him in the nude, "you sure ain't helping much. And I can't imagine what them whores in town loved about you so much. Hell, your pecker ain't no bigger than a walnut. And my Lord, are you ever fat. That hog Mr. Shepard served up last Christmas ain't got nothing on you. Hell, Momma ain't got nothing on you. Look at you, spreading all over the ground like thick porridge. It's ridiculous. Look at him, Lightning. God sure didn't bless you in the body department. Once you get to Heaven, you might want to ask for your money back on it, or however that works. Ask for your prayers back, I guess. I reckon your arms don't have much hair."

Liz Sawyer positioned herself over Father Milton's left arm, holding the Bowie knife with two hands. She came down on his upper arm hard, chopping through to the bone on one swing, blood spraying up across her face. The second chop mistakenly came down at an angle, causing the blade to ricochet off the bone and avulse a large chunk of his meaty bicep. Liz picked up this piece of filleted flesh and looked at it, a slight grin on her bloodied face. She saw the layer of skin and muscle, and the thick yellowish layer of fat. She sniffed the piece of meat—no smell, aside from minor whiff of body odor that already encompassed the priest's corpse. She tossed this piece in the fire.

She came down again on the humerus, grunting as she swung, the blade cracking against the bone, which bowed inward but didn't break. Again she chopped, and again, the muscles of her arms, back, and abdomen screaming, chips of bone and chunks of muscle and fat flying everywhere, littering the camp and getting not just on, but *in* her clothes and her hair. Liz had ceased to care. She just wanted that damn bone to break.

"I'm about give out, Lightning. You sure you can't grow no hands? You'd think cutting a man's arm off wouldn't be no big chore, but it is. What I need is a chisel and hammer, that's what I need. Lightning, go on back to town and visit Mac's and tell his drunk ass that Liz Sawyer needs a hammer and chisel. Can you do that? I'm just playing with you, Lightning. Don't go anywhere. Hell, you might run into more horse eaters out there. Best to stay close to me. Horse-eating man of God, I ain't never heard of such."

Drawing in a deep breath, Liz lifted the gore-dripping knife over her head, her eyes wide and intent on the spot of bone that appeared the weakest. She swung down, yelling as she did so, and lopped off Father Milton's arm.

"Thank Christ!" she exclaimed, panting. "I reckon I'll be sore tomorrow from all this chopping. Whew! You sure got a funny look on your face, Father—one eye looking this way, one eye looking that way, blood all over, and your mouth all wide open like you're . . . say, are you hungry, Father? That's right, you said you were hungry. Wanted to eat a horse, as I recall. Here, let me help you out. I'll feed you a walnut."

Liz reached down, grabbing the small head of the priest's penis and stretching it out. Then, with one swift slice of her Bowie knife, Father Milton was peckerless. "There we go," Liz said, holding it up in two fingers like one would do a chocolate dipped fruit. "I don't know if it will fill you up, but it'll get you started." She dropped the severed cock into Father Milton's mouth and shoved his jaw closed. "Alright, back down to business."

Liz stuck the knife in the dirt and grabbed up Father Milton's amputated arm by the hand. She sat cross-legged on the ground by the fire and held the arm over the flames, watching it begin to bubble and sear. Roasting human flesh smelled different than hog or cow, Liz decided, and wondered if it would taste different. She mused at how when she turned the arm over to cook the other side, the elbow bent. When she turned it over again, it stretched out.

"It's kinda funny holding his hand while his arm cooks," she said to Lightning. "I bet he never figured on that happening. You think eating a priest will give me any special God powers? You know, cause he's supposedly holy and God-fearing and all. I reckon not, I guess. It might put me in *wrong* with the Lord, now that I think about it. Better than eating a horse, though. There are special commandments against eating horses, I'm fairly sure. Yeah, I bet ol' Father Milton didn't wake up thinking, 'You know, I reckon I'll go ride my horse into a ravine today and then get myself chopped up and eaten by a little girl today.'"

Hours later, with her belly full and the blood dry on her face, gunshots rang out from the mountains. Liz opened her eyes only for a moment, not bothering to sit up or even stir, figuring the continued shooting was likely part of some Comanche or Kiowa ceremony. "Indians are so crazy sometimes," she whispered as her eyes closed and sleep took hold again.

PART FOUR:

THE NIGHT TRIBE

1

"**I**'VE HEARD LEGENDS," Whispering Wind said when the shooting finally ceased. "From my father and his father before him. They called them the Night Tribe."

2

(A Brief Historical Interlude)

IN THE SPRING of 1934, Harvard University Historical Press published *Mysterious Mountains: Legends and Folklore of America's Mountain Ranges*, by Christopher Michael Watts. Subsequently, an updated version of the text, with additional research and information by the author, was published in September of 1952 by Cerberus Press. The following is a chronological list of events, disappearances, and murders attributed to the so-called "Night Tribe," as described by Watts in chapter thirteen—"The Night Killers of North America."

1699: In the White Mountains in what is now New Hampshire, a fur trader named Bart Jennings returned to his cabin late on the night of October 15th to find that his family—wife Kenzie and sons Matthew and Frank—were missing. The next morning, their bodies were discovered a short ways from the cabin, dismembered and with much of the flesh eaten away. It was theorized that bears or wolves were responsible. However, Kenzie was known to make nightly journal entries, and the last two sentences of her entry for the evening of the 15th stated, "There are strange noises in the skies. Like big birds or bats."

1720: Renowned botanist Derick Miller set out to explore the Blueberry Mountain of what is now southern Maine, along with his wife, Genevieve, and four Wabanaki guides. None of them were ever seen again. During the search for the Millers and their guides, a pine tree was found to have "they were taken by the sky" etched into the trunk with a knife or rock. It was never discovered who left the message or what it meant.

1757: Two boys, Arthur Wright and Timothy Range, claimed to have slept on the roof of the capitol building in Colonial Williamsburg on a full moon night in late September, whereupon they claim to have seen giant birds flying over the hills to the west. Wright claimed that they were actually people with bird wings. Though Timothy disputed this, Arthur claimed to have seen the giant birds repeatedly picking up animals off the ground and flying off with them.

1792: In the Appalachian Mountains, explorer James Harrod went on a hunting trip in February with two other men, named Bridges and Stoner. Two weeks later, Bridges and Stoner returned from the trip, informing Harrod's family and the nearby townsfolk that Harrod had gone missing while they were away. Theories range from murder at the hands of Bridges to Indians, and even to Harrod deciding to leave his wife and start a new life elsewhere. But, according to

Stoner, the men were plagued the entire trip with things that flew around their camp at night, keeping them awake, and that one night the mule the trio had taken to transport their gear was carried away by whatever was in the sky, never to be seen again.

1805: While crossing through the Bitterroot Mountains in mid-September, the Lewis and Clark expedition came across a tribe of Salish Indians that had been decimated, apparently by war with rival tribes. However, the journal of Meriweather Lewis suggests otherwise: *"This morning we saw to the north at a distance of one mile a collection of twelve to fifteen tipis. Drewyer informed us that it was the Salish. Thus, we set out to meet this tribe of Indians. However, upon our arrival at their camp, the Salish people were in hysterics over some recent battle that had taken place. Dead Salish lay all about, with their limbs and heads removed and with flesh gone from their bodies. When Drewyer attempted to identify the culprits of this attack, the frantic Salish would only keep repeating the same thing, saying it was the "demons of the sky" and "it was the Night Tribe." We disembarked a short time later, unable to assist the grieving tribe, and with no clearer understanding of the events. We've never seen such violence."* (Note: This is the first known usage of the term "Night Tribe")

1849: The Butterworth family of Little Rock, Arkansas, along with half the nation at that time, decided to make their way west to California in search of gold. The family consisted of Bill and Jean, as father and mother, and ten children, ranging in age from two to nineteen. From all accounts, the trip was going well until the family reached the Wichita Mountains. At some point during their travels through this area, the entire family went missing, except for ten-year-old Stephanie, who appeared alone in nearby Barrier Ridge in late August, dazed and confused and claiming that the devil had carried off her entire family along with their horses. Naturally skeptical of this story, the authorities of the time speculated that the family likely traveled west without the girl, either by mistake or intentionally. However, three years later the Butterworth's wagon was discovered in the mountains, shattered and unattended to. No sign of the family has ever been discovered.

1856: The Cox brothers, George, 7, and Joseph, 5, disappeared from their family's cabin in the Allegheny Mountains on April 24th. According to their father, Samuel, the family dog had been barking towards the sky all the previous night and on the night following the disappearance, at which time the dog too disappeared. On May 7th, the bodies of both boys were found in the woods less than a mile from the cabin. According to the observations of two area physicians, it appeared the boys had fallen from a great height. The family dog was never found.

1882: Over the course of just a few days in late November in the Wichita Mountains, more than a dozen Comanche were murdered, dismembered and stripped of their flesh; a group of outlaws known as the Tate Gang, who had recently made good an escape from authorities, suffered a similar fate; and a priest, Father Roger Milton III, was killed, his left arm and leg, along with his penis, having been torturously removed. Also going missing at the same time was a teenager named Elizabeth Hughes and a mountain dweller named James Haggard, though, it is widely assumed that Haggard fled the territory after murdering his wife and daughter. There were several reports from nearby residents claiming to have heard noises in the skies and around the mountains during this time. One of these people was none other than Stephanie Hughes—formerly Stephanie Butterworth —who'd been the lone survivor of the incident in 1849, and the mother of missing Elizabeth.

1889: In an area of the Rocky Mountains that is now northern Utah, the Watsons, a Mormon family of eight, went missing in late May. A nearby trapper and fur trader named Cody Higgins, upon investigation, stated he had not seen or heard the family pass by his cabin, but all through the night in question, he heard a loud fluttering in the skies. Higgins stated he did not go outside to see what the commotion was about because, in his words, he was "shit-faced." Naturally, this called into question his account of hearing things in the sky. The Watson family was never found.

1913: Although it's widely speculated that American author Ambrose Bierce perished in the Battle of Ojinaga or some other battle in war-torn Mexico, one report by a Chihuahua newspaperman suggests that Bierce fell-in with a group of adventurers bound for the Cordillera Mountains. Less than two months later, the mutilated bodies of an estimated fifteen individuals were discovered in the mountains just under a hundred miles southwest of Chihuahua. None of the remains could be identified.

1929: On the evening of December 13th, thirty miles north of Boulder, CO, America's most prolific female hunter and outdoorsman, Chrissy Morgan, claimed to have shot and killed three pterodactyl-like creatures while hunting wolves in the mountains. However, upon returning to the site three days later accompanied by three biologists from the nearby university, no sign of the creatures remained. Morgan was later deemed a fraud and her accounts of these events considered a hoax, though, she held to her claims until her death in 1948.

1945: During a nighttime training mission departing Thompson-Robbins Field in Helena, Arkansas, the ten-man crew aboard a B-14 Liberator flying over the Ozarks reported having to conduct evasive maneuvers in order to avoid colliding with ten to fifteen "large winged animals." Captain Jon Davis reported at first thinking it was a formation of P-51 fighter aircrafts, but upon drawing closer, realized they were in fact biological in nature. The case was dismissed by the US Army Air Force, whose unofficial statement was that the crew likely mistook a flock of birds for something else.

Let it be known that the preceding accounts do not include the hundreds of unverified stories and legends of the "Night Tribe" that are prevalent in nearly every Native American culture, especially those of mountainous regions.

3

WHEN THE THING grabbed Dom Tate, Crow finally got something to aim at, and he did so, raising his Colt and firing as it lifted off the ground with Dom clutched screaming in its clawed feet.

He fired three shots in rapid succession, pulling the hammer and then the trigger as quickly as his hands would allow. Richard, too, was firing, and did so until his revolver was empty. Crow wasn't sure either of them hit the fast-moving beast until its flight faltered about forty feet into the air.

It came crashing to earth, with Dom beneath it, his ribs cracking with the impact, air rushing out of him in a pain-filled scream. The thing flung Dom from its grasp, sending him tumbling through the dust like a ragdoll. Then it turned to face Crow.

It stood at least eight feet tall and was unlike anything he'd ever seen. Stretched out, its wings displayed a span close to twenty feet; the wings were hairless and featherless, paper thin and grayish, with thick veins coursing through them. The entire creature, in fact, was dark gray, its skin heavily wrinkled and cracked in a way Crow attributed to descriptions he'd heard of elephants and rhinos. But this creature was thin, unlike those fleshy animals. Its legs were long and stork-like—the knee joint backward-pointing like a bird's—with feet consisting of four toes facing forward and one to the rear, each with a long, curved talon. It had no arms, Crow noticed, only the menacing spreading wings. Long, pointed ears sprouted from either side of its head, looking somewhat like horns.

Yet, it was the thing's face that most froze Crow with terror—round and almost humanlike, hairless like the rest of it, and encased in that odd, creased gray pruney skin. Deep, dark eye sockets housed glowing blue orbs that seemed miles away inside its skull, below which were two slits for a nose, and below those . . . the mouth. It had no lips or gums. Instead, its long fangs appeared to grow straight from the flesh of its face. None of the teeth were blunt; they were all long and sharp and dripping with saliva. As its jaws opened, Crow saw rows upon rows of more jagged fangs behind them.

Dark blood streamed from a tattered hole in one shoulder, where the muscle attached to the wing. This wound, he presumed, was what brought the creature down.

Crow took in these observations in a matter of seconds, as the creature approached. Richard tried frantically to reload while Dom crawled helplessly through the dirt, spitting up blood and as Whispering Wind, unbeknownst to anyone, grabbed the Winchester that Connor had been carrying and chambered a round. The creature's head whipped her way when she actioned the rifle, and she fired, the bullet catching it in the lower abdomen, its mouth stretching open in what appeared to be a scream of agony, though no noise was made. The sound of the rifle brought Crow out of his frozen daze. He leveled his revolver at the thing and fired his last two rounds into its chest.

The monstrosity fell to its back, its wings and legs twitching as if in the midst of a seizure.

"They're attacking the horses!" Whispering Wind shouted. The rifle she'd retrieved reported again, and Crow was impressed by the courage and fight that had suddenly emerged in her. *Where was it all this time?* he wondered.

He turned on his heels toward the area where their horses were tethered. So far from the fire, and without a glimmer of moonlight, he could barely see anything, but he heard their frantic squealing, and hooves beating the ground in decreasing numbers. He could also hear the flapping of monstrous wings, and, to his horror, the tearing and gnawing of flesh.

"Get away from our goddamn horses!" Richard ran past Crow, blasting two revolvers at once, apparently having picked up either Dom's or Noel's.

Crow followed, reloading the cylinder to his gun as he did. From behind him, Whispering Wind continued to fire, and he prayed she was taking note of where he and Richard were, though he doubted she would be bothered much by shooting either of them in the process.

Two of the beasts held a horse several feet off the ground, one with its talons digging into its hindquarters, another with its clawed feet tearing into the same horse's head. Crow wasn't sure if the monsters were fighting over the animal or trying to rip it into smaller pieces, not that it mattered. More monsters were attacking the other horses, butchering them. *Must be a dozen, at least!* he thought.

Crow shot at the beast at the horse's head—once, twice, three times. At last, it wavered, appearing injured and attempting to flee, but still with the horse's severed head in its grip. Crow changed targets, shooting his last two rounds into the second beast. It had already ripped one hind leg off, and when Crow's shots hit it center mass, it took flight with that same silent scream on its face.

He stopped again to load, panting, sweat pouring down his face despite the cold, his heart thundering against his ribcage. Richard was almost upon them now—almost in the center of the beasts and the horses. "Stop, Richard! You're too close!" Crow yelled, closing the loaded cylinder again. Gunfire was still coming from behind him, from Whispering Wind, and he saw one the monster's head's explode, its legs crumpling beneath it and its wings folding as it dropped. *Damn, she's a hell of shot,* Crow thought. *Even in the dark!*

He opened fire again, hitting one in the leg as it took to the skies with a huge chunk of meat clutched in its claws. Another took flight, and another, and Crow fired up at them, running towards what was left of the horses. He fired until his revolver was empty once more, opened the cylinder, and let the empty shell-casings drop to the dirt, his fingers trembling and grasping at ammo in his belt.

At this point, he looked around, realizing all of the gunfire, even from Whispering Wind, had ceased. So too had the sound of their horses being torn to shreds. The beasts were gone. All that was left of the horses was lifeless lumps of meat—a head here, a torso there, various organs spread all over. The rest were gone.

And, Crow realized, Richard Tate was gone too.

4

WELL, RICHARD TATE wasn't *entirely* gone.

Everything from the waist up was, however, aside from several feet of splattered tendrils splaying out from his lower half like roots from a tree. Both of his boots were missing, so Crow assumed one monster had made off with Richard's head and torso, while another took flight with nothing more than a couple of stinky leathers.

The revolvers Richard had been firing before his demise lay not far away. Crow collected these and returned to the camp, still shocked. He found Whispering Wind helping Dom Tate—who did not look to be doing well at all; worse than Noel had been, in fact—to a sitting position on a log near the fire. Dom was coughing up blood, arms cradling his chest as if his organs may fall out if he let go. Crow thought the man looked ashen—on the brink of death.

"I've heard legends," Whispering Wind said to Crow, sitting beside Dom with one arm around him, as if he hadn't raped her numerous times and called her all form of horrid names. "From my father, and his father before him. They called them the Night Tribe. My father was not fond of the Kiowa, but he told me of a time that the Comanche and Kiowa came together to fight the Night Tribe. He said they were powerful things—almost gods—that were evil, and killed man and animal alike. My grandfather—he's dead fifteen years now—taught me a saying, what you may call a nursery rhyme or a poem: When the Night Tribe is here, stay out of the hills; but you're always safe when you have the sun; it's only at night that the Night Tribe kills; only when they're full is the carnage is done."

5

JAMES HAGGARD WALKED through the night, never stopping, even as his mind became weary and restless and wanted for sleep. When Sarah and Meredith joined him on his travels, he barely found it strange.

He staggered over rocky hills, unable to see more than a few feet in front of him. Only occasionally did the clouds part and allow him the slightest glimpse of moonshine. The Winchester rifle slung over his back grew heavy. He'd thought more than once about tossing it aside. His ankles were swollen and sore from twisting on rocks he couldn't see. His hands ached from digging their graves.

"Are you okay, Daddy?"

Meredith joined him first, walking easily—almost skipping—alongside. Her hair was braided the way she liked it and she was wearing the nightgown he'd recently bought her at Mac's.

"I'm just tired," Haggard mumbled, tripping over a log and nearly falling to his knees. Meredith continued walking, unaffected by the obstacles. "It's been a long day."

"Where are you going, Daddy?"

For a moment he couldn't remember, and this

terrified him. He was on mission, that much he knew. Not the kind of mission a military man embarks on, but a mission all the same. He was searching for someone, or a group of someones. Wasn't that it? "I'm looking for someone," he said.

"Who are you looking for, hon?"

This was Sarah. She had joined him, coming up on his left while Meredith was on his right. She too was in her nightgown, with her hair braided and looking lovely.

"I don't know," Haggard whispered. "I don't remember."

"Why don't you go back home, hon?"

Her voice was pleasant and thoughtful, touching his soul as truly as a hand grasps another hand. It was as if he'd not heard her speak in ages. Like expensive silk was to the flesh, so too was Sarah's voice to his ears. Gooseflesh cropped up along Haggard's arms, and he felt his heart quicken, the hair on the back of his neck standing on end.

"Home?" he said, his feet continuing to trudge forward.

"Home, James," Sarah said. "You've done enough. You can't undo what has happened."

"Come home, Daddy," Meredith said.

"I can't undo what's happened?" Haggard said, his fatigued mind searching for what she was talking about. "What has happened?"

Silence from the two.

He looked first at Sarah, then at Meredith. But they just kept walking silently, their eyes cast straight ahead, as if focusing on something in the blackness. Haggard attempted to follow their gaze, but succeeded only in tripping over another rock, this time causing him to fall to his hands and knees. "What happened?" he said again, rolling onto his back, feeling the discomfort of the rifle beneath him. Even through his shirt and coat, he could feel how cold it was. "What happened?"

But they weren't answering. His eyes closed. And there he was again, walking into the cabin, calling for them . . . finding them, bloodied, butchered, *violated!*

His eyes shot open, tears streaming down his face. Sitting up quickly, yelling the names of his wife and daughter, he found nothing but darkness. Bringing his knees to his chest, his sobbing screams echoed off the mountains.

When his cries eventually died down, Haggard fought to his feet and staggered onward. He no longer remembered what direction the gun shots had come from, not that he knew what direction he was walking in, anyway. But he would find more of them no matter which direction he went—more of the red swine that killed his family.

And he found one at dawn, just as the sun was peeking over the hills to the east and providing the first few rays of warming light.

Where two sloping hillsides met in a depressed area of the ground, creating a small pool of water from nights of frost and days above freezing, an Indian woman was dipping a canteen into the water. Her hair obstructed Haggard's view of her face, as he approached from still fifty feet away. But her figure beneath her woolen trousers and deerskin top, and the delicate nature of her arms and hands, gave her sex away.

A SAVAGE BREED

It was wonder she had not heard him coming. Or, at least, it appeared she had not. Haggard was not attempting to silence his travels. If he spooked a bear or a coyote or bloodthirsty savage, then so be it. He would kill them until he was killed.

He continued to walk as he unslung his Winchester and pulled back the hammer. When she finally did look up, he pulled the trigger.

6

LIZ SAWYER WAS awake long before the sun rose. She was cold for one thing, even with her blanket *and* the tattered remains of Father Milton's fur coat, which turned out to have a bundle of money in its pocket—Lucky Liz! She also, if only barely, recalled hearing all the shooting that occurred at some point during the night.

But what really kept her waking up every thirty minutes or so was being worried sick that wolves or coyotes or bears or God knows what would come in the night to feast on the priest. He was too damn fat for her to haul off from the camp. She hadn't thought to bring any rope, but she reckoned she could figure out a way to have Lightning pull him away, if she put her mind to it. Dog gone it, though, when you got a full belly and you're tired from a long day of adventuring, your mind just doesn't work like you want it to.

The remains of Father Milton's arm had roasted pretty good. Liz hadn't known how long one was supposed to cook a human arm, so—better safe than sorry—she let it go good and long. Even after eating much of the bicep from around the bone, she flipped the arm over and cooked the hand too, then gnawed off the pinky, which turned out to be better tasting than the upper arm. The meal needed salt, but it wasn't bad. And hungry girls had to eat, so she didn't complain. When she felt fatter than a tick, she'd thrown the rest (there was still plenty of meat left) into her satchel.

When she woke up for the last time that night, however, she decided having a human arm in her satchel probably wasn't the best idea. What if someone came along and saw it? Not that she intended to let anyone rummage through her bag, but you never knew what could happen when you were on an adventure like this. Best to prepare for such instances. If someone found out she had an arm in her bag, then they would have questions. Hell, they might go to the law! She was perfectly in her right to shoot a horse-eating, whoring, no-good priest like Father Milton—and she was okay to eat him, too! What did people want her to do, starve to death? But trying to explain this to someone, she reckoned, would be difficult. So, Liz had taken her trusty Bowie knife and scraped off every shred of meat. It was tough and blackened on the outside and dry as August all the way through, like jerky, which to her understanding meant it wouldn't spoil for a long time. The scrumptious priest jerky went in the satchel and the naked bony arm went in what was left of the fire.

"I guess it's best we get moving," she said to Lightning, slinging the saddle on her and strapping it in place. She situated her flat-billed hat atop her head and mounted up, looking west to the mountains, not that she could see much of them before sunrise. "California awaits!" she yelled, then looked down at the body of the priest, tipping her hat at him. "It's been nice knowing you, Father. I reckon the coyots will get the rest of you. You won't go to waste. God doesn't like stuff going to waste. At least, that's what Momma said. So, who knows, really."

Liz rode slowly and quietly for a time, watching the skies as the clouds finally started to depart just before dawn, opening up a majestic view of the stars. She loved looking at the stars, wondering what was out there. Back when she was Elizabeth Hughes, she loved to climb onto the roof of her house and watch the stars while Papa and Momma slept. If only it was spring or summer instead of late fall and cold. If it was warmer out, she would hear the crickets, grasshoppers, and cicadas doing their thing. Liz loved that sound. Papa said they made those screeching noises as part of the mating process, and Liz found this truly fascinating. The male cicada could just make a funny screeching noise and some female would fly down and spread her legs for him. Not near as complicated as the mating rituals of people, Liz knew. Like the time that Mexican boy, Manny, took off his hat when she came walking by and had his hair all brushed, and then he gave her some flowers and tried to talk all poetic. He was obviously trying to mate with her! He probably didn't think his advances would lead to a broomstick in his rear and a cat running off with his foreskin, but it did.

A sliver of sun was peeking over the horizon behind her by the time Liz reached the hills, and she was thankful for the mildly warm touch it provided. The clouds were gone completely now and the sky was turning blue before her eyes, as if a master painter of the cosmos had grown weary of the stars and, with few strokes of his magical brush, was birthing the most beautiful dawn Earth had ever witnessed.

A dead horse lay in her path a little further on, with the sun truly lifting from the east hills. She halted Lightning as they came along side it, observing its throat appearing to have been torn open.

"What the devil happened here, Lightning?" she said, looking down on the dead steed from her saddle. "Father Milton preparing his dinner, I reckon. No, no, I know Father Milton was coming from the other direction. I just didn't figure on there being more than one horse-hater in these parts. Who would cut open a horse's throat that way? I ain't never heard of Indians doing such a thing, have you? That old codger Miss Jones claims she was raped and beaten by twenty-three Indians. Now, pardon me for questioning a Christian woman, but exactly how did she have the presence of mind to count them savages as they were pounding on her like a Mexican piñata and poking their peckers in every hole she had? Personally, I think that lush of a husband of hers decided to teach her a lesson or two one night, and she just didn't want to admit such a thing to her gossiping friends at the church. But anyway, I ain't never heard of Indians killing horses."

She rode on, discovering soon that there was more than just a dead horse in the hills. She came across a pile of innards next. Then there was a horse's head, with half its face gone, but no body. She was sure there must be a mad horse killer on the loose. Perhaps another priest! But then she came across an arm—a human arm! Just lying there in the dirt like somebody set it there, with bloody tissue sticking out the shoulder where it should have been attached to a body somewhere. As if someone had been walking along and their arm fell off and they just kept walking. There was no sign of a fight or anything, that Liz could see.

"Well, ain't that something," Liz said, as she and Lightning passed the arm. "What do you reckon the chances are that there would be two severed arms in such close proximity?" Lightning did not respond, but Liz figured the chances were relatively slim.

Over the next hill, things got even weirder.

It appeared as though an apocalyptic battle had taken place. Like something straight out of the Book of Revelation. Blood and guts were everywhere! Human body parts and horse body parts were strewn all over the ground.

And there were . . . these *things*! Smoldering things, as if they'd been set on fire. Kneeling next to one, presumably inspecting it, was a man, his rugged, unkempt beard and heavily bruised face giving him a menacing appearance. As Liz and Lightning appeared, he looked up.

"What the hell is that?" Liz said when she was almost upon him.

He stood, and was on the verge of saying something when a gunshot rang out.

7

SLEEP WASN'T CONCEIVABLE after the attack. Crow spent the remainder of the night cleaning and reloading firearms, and watching the skies. When the clouds at last gave way to the moon and stars, he was somewhat thankful; he would at least be able to see movement in the skies if they came back.

Typically, Crow wasn't one to ponder, but the events of the night and what happened when the sun finally shed light on those long, dark hours had him questioning everything he knew. He wasn't a Godly person, but accepted the possibility of God. Nor had he ever been intrigued by tales of the supernatural, such as ghosts or the caddja or the wendigo of the Chisholm Trail. Though he figured there was considerable lore with which he was unfamiliar, he found it odd that stories of Whispering Wind's Night Tribe had never reached his ears. If he'd heard such stories in on a whiskey boat or in a saloon, he likely would have laughed them off as the fairy tales of children, if he listened at all.

And if the teller of the tale told him that the creatures that swooped down in the night killing at will turned to smoldering ash with the first touch of sunlight, then he would have called that story teller crazy.

It'd actually been Dom Tate to first notice how the creatures' corpses were reacting to daylight. He and Whispering Wind had found some sleep, though Dom's breathing had been as rickety as an ancient rocking chair all night. Crow wouldn't have been surprised had it stopped altogether by dawn. But Dom had pulled through.

"Why's it smoking?" he asked weakly, suppressing a cough that likely would've resulted in more blood being wiped from his chin.

Crow, who'd been picking at the grime under his nails as the sun rose, initially thought Dom was talking about the fire, and was about to inform him that's what fires do—smoke—when he noticed the man's gaze and turned to look. The first creature to fall—the one that had crushed Dom—was smoldering in the spots touched by the morning sun, the end of one wing and the top of its skull. Thick white smoke billowed from the gray flesh, which appeared to be blackening and melting before his eyes. And Crow realized now that it was sizzling, like bacon on the griddle.

What the hell? Crow thought, standing up and moving closer. He saw that, as the flesh melted away from its head, the skull itself was beginning to deteriorate, cracking, turning brittle and ashy colored.

"What is happening?" Whispering Wind asked, coming up alongside him.

"Don't know," Crow said, his bruised brow crinkled in confusion. He looked to where the larger battle took place the night before, where the horses had been tethered. Two more creatures had been killed there, one by Whispering Wind and the other likely by a combination of him and Richard, and these creatures too were smoldering, even more so, as the morning sun shone greater on them.

"I guess that's why they don't come out in the day," Whispering Wind said. "We need more water. I'm going to fill the canteen. I saw a pool on the other side of the hill."

Crow nodded. He looked at Dom—whose eyes had closed as he leaned back against a log, his chest resuming the painful breathing pattern it had displayed all night—then over at the smoldering beasts among the slaughtered horses, and decided to take a closer look.

The sun was almost fully over the horizon as he crouched beside what was left of one the creatures. Its flesh was nearly completely gone, having liquefied and gathered beneath the skeleton in a bubbling mess that resembled tar. The odor it emitted was like something between boiled eggs and mud, though Crow, having lived with eight other men on a whiskey boat, was unaffected by the smell. The bones looked a million years old, not a single one free of cracks and splinters. The organs once protected by these bones were quickly melting away, as well.

Reaching out, Crow touched what had been one of the thing's ribs. It fell away in a cloud, like powder.

Then he heard hoofbeats approaching, and his head shot up. He saw an oddly familiar white horse coming his way, with a young girl riding.

"What the hell is that?" she said, bringing the horse to a halt.

As baffling as the melting monsters were, Crow

wondered what a girl of maybe twelve or thirteen was doing out here in the mountains. He stood, sweeping the bone powder from his hands, about to tell her he didn't have the slightest idea, but that she'd best ride on back where came from, when a gunshot echoed through the hills.

Crow whipped around, instinctively pulling the Colt from his holster. *That came from the direction Whispering Wind went*, he thought. Though he still felt she would have been better off if he'd killed her in East Texas where he found her, he had to admit he'd grown fond of her. Not, perhaps, in a romantic way. She was beautiful, yes, Crow wouldn't deny that. But it was her resolve he found most impressive. That, and her unbelievable tenderness towards an injured man who'd been so cruel to her.

He bolted that way, forgetting about the disintegrating creatures and the girl on the white horse. He tore past the camp, where Dom lay apparently oblivious. Rather than going around the hill as Whispering Wind had done, he sprinted up it in long thigh-burning strides. It was a small, rocky hill with very little foliage, the soil having a tendency to shift under one's foot. Vaguely, Crow heard the horse following, but did not much care.

Reaching the crest of the hill, he fell to his belly, pointing his revolver down the other side as the scene came into view.

Whispering Wind was kneeling, facing away from Crow, beside a pool of water. Standing in front of her was a man holding a lever action rifle at his waist, the barrel pointing at her head. He appeared to be saying something. Though Crow could not hear because of the breeze and the distance, the expression on the man's face suggested he was not inquiring if Whispering Wind knew the nearest place to get a drink and a shave.

Crow took aim at the man, but possessed little confidence he could hit him at such range and angle. In fact, he was just as likely to accidentally hit the woman. He reckoned he had two choices: either attempt to sneak closer so as to have a better shot, or could stand up and present himself and perhaps try to reason with the man. Both plans were flawed. With the rifle in hand, the mystery man held the advantage, even if Crow retained the element of surprise.

He was on the verge of standing, intending to say something along the lines of 'Good morning, stranger' (it was all he could think of), when the man appeared suddenly distracted, looking to his right as if hearing something.

Then, from around the side of the hill, came the brilliant white horse and the girl who rode it. In her lap she cradled a rifle of her own, its brass receiver gleaming with the morning sun.

What the hell is she doing? Crow thought, wondering again who the hell she was and why she was complicating an already complicated situation. For all he knew, she might be with the man who currently held Whispering Wind captive. *Probably his daughter*, Crow thought.

The girl guided the horse lazily up to the pool of water, where it bent down for a drink. She was saying something to the man, who seemed confused by her presence—he just stood gawking at her. She made lively hand gestures, as if telling some detailed tale that required visualizations. And . . . she was laughing. Her face became yet more animated as she talked, going on and on, as if taking no notice of Whispering Wind. The man with the rifle kept staring queerly at her, like he hadn't the foggiest idea what she was talking about, what she was doing there, and what he was supposed to do about her.

Whispering Wind apparently noticed the man's distraction and decided to take advantage of it. She sprang to her feet, wielding the tin canteen with two hands as if it were a club, and struck him hard on the side of the head. He fell straight backward, making no effort to break his fall or soften the impact, instantly knocked out. As he lay there unmoving, Crow saw the laughing girl giving Whispering Wind a thumbs-up.

8

TOGETHER, CROW AND Whispering Wind dragged the man by the boots around the hill and back to their camp, not caring that his back and head were probably being shredded in the process.

For some reason, Whispering Wind had handed off both the man's guns—the rifle and a revolver—to the girl on the horse before Crow reached the scene. He didn't feel comfortable with someone he didn't know being so well armed, but first things first; he needed to deal with this mystery man.

They dropped his heels in the dirt not far from where Dom continued to doze in and out of sleep—or consciousness—with his rattling chest and frequent agonizing moans. Dom was another problem that would likely need solving soon.

"We need to tie this fella up before he comes to," Crow said, going over to what had been Connor's bedroll until he was hauled off to his death in the skies. There was a rope around the bedroll, which Crow removed.

"I can tie him up," said the girl, dismounting. She tethered the white horse, slid her own rifle into a saddle-holster, and gave the mystery man's rifle to Crow. His revolver, she kept in her belt along with another holstered Colt. "I'm really good at tying folks up. Good at tying anything up, I reckon." She held her hand out as if it were a foregone conclusion that Crow would relinquish the rope. He did.

Whispering Wind settled on the log next to Dom, looking at him with concern and placing a hand on his shoulder. The sun was full in the east now, with not a cloud in its way, though the morning still bore a chill, assisted by a breeze. The creatures were all but gone, their bodies and skeletons having dissolved into what could easily be mistaken for the ash from an extinguished fire. Even their smell was gone.

Crow watched as the girl began tying the mystery man's hands together with a quickness and ease that was beyond impressive. When his hands were bound tight (it looked to Crow as if he would find difficulty sliding a piece of newspaper between the man's wrists), the girl produced a Bowie knife and cut off the remainder of the rope, then used it to bind the man's feet and ankles in the same fashion.

"Where'd you learn that?" Crow said.

"School, of course. Isn't that where you're supposed to learn things?" the girl responded, slapping her hands together and looking down at the knots with pride.

"I didn't go to school," Crow said. "They teach you how to tie rope like that in school?"

"Well, no. I taught myself, I reckon. But I learned at school. How else was I supposed to keep them other kids from getting away? The teacher wasn't too happy that day, I tell you what."

Crow raised an eyebrow but said nothing more. He wasn't sure what to think of her yet. She was odd.

And that horse, now he had a moment to think about it, bore a striking resemblance to the one Sheriff Hughes had been sitting atop when he took a bullet to the head.

Turning to Whispering Wind, he said, "How is he?" referring to Dom.

"Not well." She shrugged. "I don't think he can travel. Certainly not without a horse. A wagon would be preferable."

For him to go ahead and die would be preferable, Crow thought, but didn't say. The squaw had a far kinder heart than he. The Tates as a whole were no friends to him, but simply business partners, of a sort. If he were broken beyond repair, laid on a log and unable to walk two feet, Crow had no doubt they would either put a bullet in him or simply walk off, leaving him to suffer until Death came to collect. They certainly wouldn't tend to his needs and give him sips of water and let him disrupt their travels, especially if there was good reason to keep moving.

And Crow believed, in this case, there *was* good reason to keep moving. For one, the law was surely to be after them. They may have killed most or all of the lawmen of Barrier Ridge, but it wouldn't be long before marshals and bounty hunters were out for blood; the price on their heads would be a massive sum now. But he was even more concerned about the creatures from the previous night returning. He didn't have the slightest idea what classification of animal they were or where they came from or what their typical sleeping and eating habits were, but there was one thing he did know: they were at the top of the food chain.

Maybe the things flew off and were a hundred miles away by now. On the other hand, maybe they found a little cavern close by and were just waiting until sunset to finish off what they'd left from the night before. Either way, Crow figured it would be best if he and Whispering Wind got moving. If the creatures came back, they could have their fun with Dom and the two strangers, for all he cared.

"What's with all these pieces of horses laying around?" the girl suddenly asked. She took a seat on a rock close to the now depleted fire. "Don't tell me y'all are horse killers. I reckon I wouldn't like being associated with no horse killers. And I reckon my girl Lightning over there wouldn't like it much either." She raised an eyebrow at Crow, having directed her question at him.

"What's your name?" Crow said, settling to the ground and resting his arms on his knees. "And what are you doing out this way?"

"I'm Liz Sawyer and I'm on my way to California, not that it's any of your business."

"What are you, twelve?"

"I am fifteen years old, thank you very much! And considering I just saved your Indian friend from being shot in the face while you was hiding behind a rock, I think you should show me a little more respect. Hell, she would have crows picking at her right now if it weren't for me coming up and telling that fella about what happened when I threw a bag full of snakes into a tipi!"

"I was not hiding." Crow looked to Whispering Wind for help, but she only shrugged, as if to say she wanted no part of this conversation. "I was . . . creeping up on him. I had it under control."

"Under control? Like hell! Anyway, what's your name, mister creeper? Next time you have the dumb idea to go running up a hill with a pistol in a rifle fight, I'd like to be able to ridicule you by name."

Crow shook his head, looking at the dirt between his legs. He couldn't help but be amused by this girl's tenacity and spunk. "I'm Crow, and this here is Whispering Wind."

Whispering Wind nodded at the girl and said, "Thank you for your help."

"I'm Dom," Dom Tate said. His head was up and he was smiling, a trickle of blood leaving the corner of his mouth. His eyes looked weary and his ashen complexion suggested that he was losing a great deal of blood, likely in his chest. "What's your name, little girl?"

"As I said a moment ago, I'm Liz Sawyer and I'm on an adventure to California. Now, are y'all going to explain to me why there are dead horses everywhere and a crumpled up dead guy over there and a man's legs over there? What the devil happened here? And what were them things when I came riding up that were all smoking?"

Crow sighed and began explaining, as best he could, the events of the night before. Though, him not being the best teller of stories and the girl, Liz, apparently being an incredibly curious individual, it led to an extended session of jabbering that frustrated Crow. Where did the monsters come from? Why were they eating horses? How old did he think they were? Did he think they'd be back tonight? Why did they dissolve in the sun? Did he think they were related to bats? Or maybe were they dinosaurs? Could there be any of them in California?

Crow didn't have answers to any of her questions. Whispering Wind offered little help either, and Dom sat listening intently as if all this was news to him.

"I tell you what I woulda done," Liz Sawyer said. "I woulda lassoed every cotton-picking one of 'em and then tied them to that tree over there. Then, when the sun came up—poof!" She added a visual hand gesture to this last part, as a magician might do upon making something disappear.

"Don't think it would be that simple," Crow said.

"Well, I do! I could always shoot 'em, too! I'm a hell of a shot, believe it or not. My Papa taught me well. I can shoot the head off a chicken!"

"Where is your father, anyway? For that matter, where is your family? No offense, Liz, but you're a trifle young to be traveling to California alone."

"Not that it's any of your business, Mister Crow, but my Papa died yesterday and my mother is a fat cow and lazier than a dead dog and scared to step outside the house unless she's walking her big behind to church. I don't reckon she would care to accompany me on my adventures, and I wouldn't much want her to, anyhow."

"Goodness, you shouldn't speak of your own mother so," Whispering Wind said.

"I'm sorry to hear of your loss," Crow said, glancing over at the white horse and wishing he hadn't asked.

"That's alright, Crow. Everyone has to die, I reckon. What matters is what you do with your life. That's what Father Milton said last Sunday, anyway. For a drunk, whore-happy, horse-eater, he could still say some smart things on occasion. Anyway, Papa was the sheriff of these parts. Sheriff Rutherford Hughes! If there was a bandit that needed hanging, well, he got 'em hanged!"

Crow and Whispering Wind sat in an awkward silence . . . but not Dom—he burst out laughing. Blood trickled from his mouth and he winced, holding his chest with both hands, as if his chuckling was causing unprecedented pain, but he didn't stop. *Stop the goddamn laughing, Dom*, Crow thought, and briefly considered pistol-whipping the man before he could say anything.

"What the devil is so funny?" Liz said.

"He's delirious," Whispering Wind said.

"His injuries have him acting mad," Crow added, sounding less than sure of himself; he'd never been a good liar.

"Your daddy was . . . Sheriff Hughes?" Dom said between sputtering bloody laughs.

"Dom, why don't you take a rest?" Crow said, more forcefully. He got to his feet, glaring at the man fiercely, trying to *will him* to shut the hell up.

"That's right," Liz said, a stern look on face. "What do you know about him?"

"What do I know?" More laughing.

"Dom!" Crow said.

"I know my brother shot that stupid prick right in the head, that's what I know!"

With a quickness Crow could hardly believe possible, Liz Sawyer sprang from the rock she was perched on, drawing the Colt and leveling it at Dom Tate. Before any of them could protest, she pulled the trigger. The gunshot cracked, the bullet tearing a hole through Dom's already battered chest.

Liz's left hand pulled the mystery man's revolver from her belt as her right thumb yanked back the hammer of her Colt. She pointed one gun at Crow and the other at Whispering Wind.

"Are y'all the Tate Gang?" she screamed. "Is that who you fuckers are? Are y'all the goddamned *Tate Gang*?"

9

WHEN JAMES HAGGARD'S eyes pried open, he saw blue skies. His head throbbed and he felt like he was spinning, as if a quart of whiskey was in his gut, working its magic. He heard someone screaming shrilly, but his boggled brain wasn't making sense of the words.

He struggled to sit up, but found his hands tied together, and had to wiggle like a beetle on its back for a moment before working himself upright.

Sure enough, some girl was shrieking about something. Haggard saw that she held a revolver in each hand and was pointing them at an Indian bitch and an ugly bearded fella. Beyond them, he saw the remnants of what looked to be a massacre of horses and people—eerily reminiscent of the scene Raging Fire had shown him.

The woman was the one who'd been filling her canteen when he shot at her and missed. As she'd cowered with fear this same girl had arrived on horseback, her mouth moving as fast as the legs of a desert cuckoo.

And then . . . nothing.

Obviously, he'd been clubbed unconscious—that's why his head was pounding like the drums from a ceremony of savages. He realized that not only his hands but his feet were bound, tight too. His guns were gone, of course. In fact, he thought the girl was holding his revolver and had it pointed at the squaw.

But Haggard still felt the knife he'd taken from that dead Indian in his coat pocket. And Meredith's handkerchief doll was still pinned to his coat, too. God help him if he ever lost that. As his mind cleared, the girl's words came into focus.

"Crow, you touch that goddamned gun and I'll shoot you and this cunt! Don't tempt me!" the girl screamed. "Actually, I change my mind. Pull your pistol out with the ends of thumb and forefinger, nothing more! Then toss it over here! You try anything funny and I'm killing the both of you!" The girl had balls, Haggard deduced.

"I'm not gonna try anything funny," the man with the beard said. He pulled the revolver from his holster as instructed and flung it to the ground at the girl's feet. "You don't have to do this, Liz."

"Ha! You can lick my ass, Crow! Y'all *are* the Tate Gang, ain't ya? Bunch of no good murdering bandits!"

"The Tates are dead," Crow said. "You just killed the last one." He nodded toward a dead man laying over the log with a bloody hole in his chest.

"Y'all are still part of the gang!"

"I was, yes. But not Whispering Wind. She did not willfully ride with us."

Whispering Wind—where had Haggard heard that name?

"Oh, so you like to kidnap Indian tramps and have your way with them, do you? Y'all are a real sweet bunch!"

Haggard suddenly realized that this squaw was the kidnapped daughter of that lousy, murdering old man he'd killed the day before.

"Not him," the squaw said. "Not Crow. He is not like the Tate brothers or the Irishman. He is a good man."

"Like hell! It's funny how everyone turns into such good folks when they have a gun pointed at them." Haggard wondered if this wasn't her first time with people at gunpoint. " I think I would trust *this* dirty bastard first—" She indicated Haggard and was now looking over her shoulder at him. Crow and the filthy Indian were looking at him too.

"Don't mind me," he said. "I'm just enjoying the show. Feels like I'm at the theater."

The girl backed up a few steps to get a better angle at them all, scooting the gun on the ground with her heel so it came with her. "Who the hell are you, anyway?" she said. "Are you one of the Tate Gang, too?"

"Little girl, I don't even know what the Tate Gang is."

"Listen here, the last person to call me 'little girl' is dead right over there. If you say it again, you join him in the afterlife. The name is Liz Sawyer. Now, who the devil *are* you and what are you doing here?"

"James Haggard. I live in the mountains north of Barrier Ridge. In fact, think I've seen you in town a time or two. As for what I'm doing here, I'm hunting Indians like that redskin bitch right there. Yeah, you! My wife and daughter were murdered by your kind two nights past, and I aim to kill every Indian I come across for the rest of my days."

Liz Sawyer stood silent for a moment, looking from Haggard to the squaw to Crow, then back to Haggard. "Your wife and daughter got killed, huh?"

"That's right."

"And you're out for revenge, is that it?"

"I'm out for justice."

"And killing every Indian you see is justice?"

"Is killing Crow justice when the man who killed your father is already dead?" the squaw said.

"You, shut up!" Liz screamed, then turned back to Haggard. "Is that your daughter's doll pinned to your coat?"

"It is," he said, looking down at it. "She carried it everywhere."

"It's got blood on it," Liz said.

Haggard's head lowered. "Would you mind untying me?" he asked under his breath.

"I think not, Mr. Haggard. I like you just how you are. I like everyone just how they are." Liz then took a couple of steps to her left and kicked what looked to be Haggard's Winchester, which had been leaned against a rock, over to the same area as Crow's revolver. "There any more guns here?"

"Yes," Crow said. "Four more pistols and another rifle over there on that blanket. I was cleaning and loading them a little while ago."

"Goddamn! What was y'all planning on doing, robbing some banks and killing some more sheriffs? Maybe you wanted to ride over to Fort Sill and knock you off some artillery soldiers while you're at it!"

"Listen, Liz," Crow said calmly, holding his hands open towards her, "I know you're upset about your father, and I understand that. But I'm not like those

Tate boys. I fell in with them to make some money, enough to hold me over for a while as I traveled the country. The truth is, when your father and his men had us lined up yesterday morning, I had accepted my fate. I didn't even know the Tates still had guns on them. I was surprised as anyone to survive yesterday morning. But here I am. And the Tate Gang is dead. I'm just a traveler again. A traveler who means you no harm. And Whispering Wind, here, certainly means you no harm. She shouldn't have been lined up with us to begin with. That priest who took her and used her like a common whore turned her in with the rest of us, like she was part of the gang."

"Father Milton turned y'all in?" Liz said, her eyes suddenly wide.

"That's right. And he said she was *with* us."

"That old drunkard never was too bright. He ran a horse straight into a ravine, believe it or not. And he ain't too Godly either, if you ask me. What kind of priest spends church funds on whores and whiskey? Anyway, he's dead now. And you would be too, if Papa had done it my way. But Momma made him stop having public hangings because I *got off* on it." She made quotes with her fingers when she said 'got off.'

Crow looked at Whispering Wind oddly, then back to Liz. "What do you say you let us just be on our way? I really don't—"

"I don't think I'm quite there yet, Crow. You just keep your seat."

"What about my ropes?" Haggard said.

"I ain't untying your ropes right now either!"

"Liz," Crow said, "if those things come back—"

"I said I ain't quite there yet!"

Crow nodded, as if to say 'very well,' then stretched out on the ground, crossing his feet and covering his face with his hat. Liz glared over at Haggard with distrust.

"I reckon I could use a nap, too," he said. Then he scowled at the squaw. "Just don't let that bitch do anything crazy." He laid back, placing his knotted hands behind his head, where he could secretly work at the knot.

"I don't think he likes you," Liz said, turning to Whispering Wind. "You seem alright to me. What kind of Indian is you?"

"I'm Comanche," she said.

"Comanche, huh? Can I ask you something about Comanches?"

Whispering Wind nodded.

"Is it true y'all are all inbred?"

10

TO HIS SHOCK, it was hours before Crow awoke.

He shot up to a sitting position, his hat falling from his face, and saw the sun already in the western sky. To his left, the mystery man, James Haggard, was still on his back with his hands behind his head and his eyes closed.

Liz and Whispering Wind were not by the dead fire. Hearing laughter from behind him, he whipped his head around. They were sitting on the blanket with all the guns and ammo in piles in front of them, along with playing cards.

"Well, look who decided to wake up," Liz said. Crow noticed that she was now wearing a blue dress and her hair was done up in braided pigtails. "I found cards in one of the saddle bags of them dead horses. You want to play? We're gambling with bullets."

"Not particularly. I want to get away from here before sunset."

"Getting away from here. Yeah, I've been thinking about that."

"Why'd y'all unload all the guns?"

"We didn't. There are still two loaded, in case you or that Haggard fella decide to go running off."

"Is that right?" Crow said, getting warily to his feet. "So, I'm your captive?"

"I didn't say that. I just like shooting at moving targets." Liz smiled at him, then looked down at her hand of cards, planning her next move. "You sure pick a bad time to rise from the grave. Whispering Wind plays cards about as good as a strangled baby takes a breath, and I'm about to win a whole bunch of ammo."

"You said you've been thinking about something. What is it?"

"Since you ask, I was thinking you and her and Mr. Haggard should all come with me to California."

"Haggard?" Crow glanced over at the man, thinking she must be joking. "He'll gut Whispering Wind the second he has a chance. You heard what he said."

"He's just cranky over losing his family. I can understand that. But he won't hold it against her long if we give him a little time. Hell, it wasn't her that killed his family! She was getting poked in the cunt by Father Milton's tiny pecker and then being turned over to the law as part the Tate Gang! Anybody with a lick of sense can see she ain't a sorry, no good bandit like you."

"Liz, I don't think it's a good idea. If you want me and Whispering Wind to join you . . . I don't know, maybe. But this Haggard fella—"

"I ain't gonna hurt the squaw," James Haggard said, still laying on his back with his eyes closed. He brought his hands down from behind his head; they were still bound tight. "You have my word, Liz, Crow, I won't hurt her."

"See, Crow," Liz said. "He's reasonable."

"You don't know that. Load my Colt and hand it here, if you don't mind."

"Oh, now you want your gun back?"

"I said, 'if you don't mind.'"

"Well, say 'please.'"

Crow's brow crinkled as he looked at her, trying to decide if she was serious. Apparently, she was. Strange little girl. Crow was not sure she was all there in the skull. She could be quick-witted, but she didn't seem to have a filter of any sort between her brain and her mouth. The way she'd executed Dom without pause, he figured it was the same with her actions.

"Please, load my gun and hand it here," he said.

Liz smiled like she'd just been handed a bag of gold coins, then started loading his revolver.

"Whoever tied these ropes did a damn fine job," Haggard said. "Was that you?" he asked Crow.

"It was Liz. I'll cut you out of them in a minute, once I have my Colt. And you're gonna move slow until we get a feel for you being untied, you understand? I will not hesitate to shoot you dead."

"You have my word," Haggard said. "To be honest, it's been a long spell since I had any grub and my stomach is grumbling. Would y'all happen to have any food?"

Crow was about to inform him that they did not when Liz spoke up.

"I have some jerky in my satchel."

"And what's with all these dead horses and body parts lying about?" Haggard said.

11

LIZ SAWYER, wearing her checkered blue dress, rode Lightning west, slow and easy, so her posse could keep up. She was amazed at how easy it was for a girl to get what she wanted when she held guns in her hand. No wonder Momma, that fat old witch, hadn't wanted her to have one.

Of course, she'd given the squaw, the bandit, and even the mourning, vengeful Mr. Haggard their guns back. Crow had protested against this last one, but finally relented after Haggard swore about twenty times not to act foolish. Now, for her trip to California, Liz had an Indian woman that could braid her hair and make fancy clothing and satchels and things out of all types of animal hide—maybe even people hide, who knows!—and who claimed she could cook, as well; and she had Crow, who, although ugly and lanky, seemed tough, cunning, and protective; and she had Haggard, who was fearless, because everything he lived for was taken from him. He would probably need to be killed at some point down the line—either for causing trouble with Whispering Wind or whining too much about his dead family or for simply being the odd man out if they ran out of food—but that could wait, Liz reckoned.

"What is this, anyway? Tastes funny," Crow said, chewing on a tough piece of priest jerky as they descended another hill in what seemed like an endless procession of them, the sun dipping halfway below the horizon ahead.

"It's meat," Liz said. "You complaining?"

"I reckon not."

"How in the hell did you get another piece?" Haggard said, walking a few yards away from the others, his revolver in its holster and his Winchester in his hands, the handkerchief doll still pinned to his coat.

"It was in my pocket. I saved it."

"Between you and that squaw, I'd be surprised there is a shred of jerky left."

Liz shot a glance over her shoulder at Haggard. "Did wittle Mr. Haggard not get enough to eat? Is him's tummy growling?"

"I could eat some more," he said, glaring.

"Well, hell, why didn't you say so? I got some more jerky. Can you believe him, Whispering Wind? Fancies himself an Indian killer, but can't ask for a second piece a meat."

"Don't talk about me that way to no squaw."

Liz reached behind the saddle and into her satchel, finding a rather large piece of priest jerky—likely a chunk of forearm—and tossing it to Haggard. He missed it and it landed on the ground, and he cursed and picked it up, brushing the dirt away. Slinging his rifle over his back, he pulled a knife from his coat pocket and began cutting away slivers of meat and sweeping them into his mouth.

"You know what I'm gonna do when we get to

California and find a bunch of gold?" Liz asked, but didn't wait for an answer. "I'm gonna buy a whole bunch of land and bunch of horses. And then I'm gonna round up all the vagrants—you know, them folks that ain't no good for society and such—and make them take good care of my horses and make them plant all kinds of crops and such, until I have the biggest and best ranch in America. And if them vagrants don't do as I say, well, I'll have all sorts of ways to take care of that. I'll have 'em whipped and caned and have their arms and legs tied to two horses pulling in opposite directions. If the men are no good, then I'll have their peckers chopped off and put in jar of pickles. And if the ladies don't want to work, then I'll have red-hot branding irons shoved up their cunts. And every Saturday night I'll make some of the vagrants fight each other to the death, and people can pay to come watch it happen. Won't that be fun?"

"That sounds an awful lot like slavery," Haggard said. "I'm pretty sure there was a war that ended with such things being outlawed."

"Mr. Haggard, you don't know nothing about history, do you? That Civil War only outlawed slavery in *southern* states. It had nothing to do with California. I think I want all my vagrant slaves to be midgets. Wouldn't that be fun? I wonder if I could find enough of 'em. They might not be too good at handling horses, though."

"Where did you get that?" Whispering Wind suddenly cried.

Liz drew Lightning to a stop, turning to look at Whispering Wind, who was pointing her rifle at

Haggard, a look of rage on her face. Crow stopped too, pulling his revolver but not pointing it anywhere yet.

Haggard froze in his tracks, in mid-chew, with a piece of priest jerky dangling off the end off his knife just in front of his face.

"What the hell are you talking about?" he said.

"That knife!" Whispering Wind screamed. "Where did you get that knife?"

Haggard's brow furrowed and he looked at the knife curiously, as if he couldn't remember where he got it, the piece of meat falling from the blade to the ground. "I found it," he said. "Yesterday, whilst walking."

"You're lying!" Whispering Wind yelled, pulling back the hammer on the rifle.

"Whispering Wind, hold on a second," Crow said, raising an open hand toward her. "What's going on here?"

"Where'd you find the knife, Mr. Haggard?" Liz said, extremely curious. "Ol' Whispering Wind seems to recognize it."

"Put the gun down," Crow said, "we can straighten this out."

Liz found this comment particularly amusing, seeing as Crow hadn't wanted Haggard tagging along to begin with.

"You're goddamned right I recognize that knife," Whispering Wind said. "It's my father's."

Liz gasped and saw Crow's eyes go wide. Haggard was about to die much sooner than she'd anticipated.

Crow slowly raised his revolver. "Where *did* you get that knife, Mr. Haggard?"

"Yeah, Mr. Haggard," Liz chimed in, smiling. "Where'd you get it?"

Only the edge of the sun shown on the horizon now, stars already twinkling in the deep blue sky. Somewhere in the distance a coyote howled and a dozen more howled back. The moon was rising in the east, bright like a lantern.

Haggard's face darkened. He grimaced with gritted teeth.

"You see this cut on my chin? This knife put it there, courtesy of an old Indian who thought his bones were quicker than they were."

"What?" Whispering Wind said, her eyes wide and shining with tears even in the failing light.

"This knife may have been the one to kill my family, too. Old man was just as crazy as you and Crow, shoveling the same shit, telling me about demons from the sky killing his whole pathetic tribe. Well, except for him and two others, but I took care of them too!"

In a blink, Haggard had dropped the knife and swung his rifle around, aiming at Whispering Wind. She, meanwhile was crying and shaking, struggling to keep her own rifle leveled at him.

"Put the gun down!" Crow also had his gun aimed at Haggard.

"Screw you, Crow."

"Mr. Haggard, if you shoot my squaw, then I'll kill you," Liz saidraising her own revolver.

"Not if I kill you first, little girl."

Hadn't she warned him not to call her that again? Liz had endured about enough of the man, but she wanted to tell him something before she killed him— enlighten him a bit.

She was about to do so when a raspy, rustling sound came from above.

A SAVAGE BREED

The four of them—armed and seeing red—looked up.

The sun was gone. Although there were no clouds, the skies were not empty.

12

UNLIKE THE PREVIOUS NIGHT, the lack of clouds and the presence of moon and stars made them visible. The creatures were high for now—the raspy sound their wings made, barely audible—but they were clearly circling them, the way vultures do a dead animal. Crow was the first to fire, the flash of his firearm briefly illuminating his menacing face. The gunshot boomed through the hills, and, as if signaling the beginning of a sporting event, it propelled the others to action.

James Haggard shouldered his Winchester and aimed it skyward, still not fully believing what he was seeing. He pulled the trigger when one of the things was in his sights, worked the lever, and fired again. Like he'd seen hawks and other birds of prey do a thousand times before, it dove toward him, picking up speed. As it neared its target, it turned, allowing its clawed feet to lead the way.

Haggard didn't move until the last second. Instead, his hands worked the lever action rifle as fast and accurately as possible—chambering a round, lining up the shot center mass, pulling the trigger, and repeating, until all six shots were spent. Only then did he step aside, allowing the creature to come crashing to the ground beside him as he unholstered his revolver and plugged one more bullet into it

"What the hell is that?" he yelled, then commenced shooting overhead again without waiting for an answer.

Liz, holding her Papa's former Colt with two hands, fired into the air, though the things moved with such speed that she wasn't sure she was hitting anything. Lightning skittered beneath her, obviously frightened. Liz squeezed the horse with her thighs as she fired at the Night Tribe, the only thing she could think to do to keep Lightning calm; it wasn't working. When the Colt was spent, she tossed the revolver aside and pulled out the Henry rifle.

Crow fired the last two shots he had into a creature as it dived upon them, the final one taking off the top of its skull. It tumbled across the ground, its leathery gray skin tearing and its brittle wings breaking as it collided with the stony face of a hill. Seeing the guns Liz had wedged under the saddle of her horse, Crow grasped two more and turned them to the sky.

Haggard downed another as it flew low, circling them.

Whispering Wind went to a knee, taking her time as she lined up one shot after another. More of the Tribe dipped from on high, her sights were on them and she fired. All her shots were true. Six shots and six hits, and at least two kills;, they plummeted, spinning as they did so, like fledgling birds. Quickly, she reloaded, her hands working frantically, her mind worried about what she could no longer see. And yet, there was part of her that knew she would save one bullet, even if it meant her life. She would save one bullet for the man who had killed her father.

But as she finished loading and worked the lever, chambering the first round, Whispering Wind looked up and saw the claws of the beast that would kill her come down. It crushed her into the ground, its talons puncturing her chest and face—one of them piercing her eye socket and delving into her brain—and then lifted off with her in its grasp, its fang-filled mouth in a kind of grin.

"Noooo!" Crow yelled, firing both revolvers at the departing creature.

One swooped toward Crow, but Haggard shot it in the face, and it glided harmlessly over the top of them before crashing into the hillside.

Liz was flung from Lightning's saddle as one of the creatures grabbed the horse by the hindquarters and began a slow ascent with the heavy Andalusian. The horse thrashed, legs trying to run without ground, head and tail whipping back and forth.

"Let go of my horse!" Liz screamed, finding her way to her feet and aiming the Henry at the creature. She fired and hit.

The horse dropped from the clutching claws. Liz was hopeful, if only for a split second, that Lightning would survive the fall. But another of the Night Tribe soared past, catching Lightning by the neck and ripping her head off.

"Noooo!" Liz screamed with tears in her eyes, as it tossed the horse's head into its mouth and flew high again. "That's my horse!" She raised her rifle again, firing at the one that killed Lightning until she was out of ammo. If she hit the monster, she never saw it come down. Reaching into the pocket of her dress, she reloaded the rifle with the last of her ammo .

Haggard barely noticed Whispering Wind's death or Lightning being snatched out from under Liz. His eyes were on his attackers. Any that flew towards him or even looked his direction got a bullet. He spent his revolver once and reloaded and spent it again, knocking down several of the Night Tribe. But when he searched his belt and his pockets for ammunition once more, he found none.

When he turned his stare skyward again, it was with a knife in his right hand—the knife of Raging Fire, father of Whispering Wind. "Come and get me, you bastard," he said, as another dove.

It was faster than him. Sweeping down, it grabbed Haggard by the shoulder. He screamed and swung erratically with the knife, slicing the thick, wrinkled flesh of its ankle. But this caused it to tighten its grip, talons pushing through the meat of his shoulder and upper chest. As it jerked away from his cuts, it tore his arm from his body and took to the skes.

"Aaaahhhh!" Haggard screamed, dropping the knife, his hand instinctively clutching for the missing arm, his legs beating at the ground as incomprehensible pain enveloped him.

But, as blood poured from his shoulder, he felt the pain seeping out of him too. He stared helplessly at the winged creatures that continued to circle. Remembering the handkerchief doll pinned to his coat—Meredith's doll—he clutched it his bloody hand and thought of Meredith and Sarah and of seeing them on the other side.

Liz, as she finished reloading her Henry, saw this

happen—saw Mr. Haggard lose his arm and writhe in pain and then apparently come to terms with his impending demise. She looked quickly skyward, making sure no creature was currently in pursuit of her, then trotted over to Haggard and knelt beside him, drawing her knife from her belt.

"Mr. Haggard, I want you to know something," she said, a gentle smile on her face. "It was me who killed your family."

His wide eyes looked intently into hers, his hand trembling so the doll shook.

"I couldn't sleep that night and needed something to do," Liz went on. "I think your wife enjoyed it when I fucked her cunt with this here Bowie knife. They both kept hollering for you. Ain't that a coincidence, that now, here we are?" Smiling down at his horrified expression, Liz buried the Bowie knife in his chest, his blood spraying across her face.

Standing back up, she turned her rifle to the heavens.

"It's just me and you, Crow!" she said. "Just me and you."

"Give 'em hell, Liz!" Crow yelled, a revolver firing in each hand. "Let's kill these fucking bastards! Let's give 'em hell!"

They did.

EPILOGUE:

A SAVAGE BREED

IF THERE HAD been eyes to see the sunrise on certain parts of the Wichita Mountains the next morning, they would have found thirteen winged creatures smoldering and melting into the ground.

They would have found a headless horse, and a one-armed man, before the coyotes found him and spread his pieces throughout the hills.

And if they looked a little further west, where the mountains finally tapered into little more than bumps in the prairie, they would have seen a bruised and bearded, lanky man and a young girl in a blue dress and a flat-billed hat, walking and talking.

"You reckon we can find many midgets in California? I like midgets. There used to be this midget in Barrier Ridge, but he drowned in a horse trough. He sure did look funny trying to come up for air. At least, that's what I heard. Anyway, you think there are many midgets in California?"

"I don't have any idea?" Crow said. "I ain't ever seen a midget. Why are you so dead set on going to California, anyhow?"

"For the adventure of it, for one. Hell, Crow, we're like Daniel Boone or Lewis and Clark or all kinds of other adventurers. Plus, I want to find some gold and get rich. Momma said we got to watch out for outlaws and chinks, though."

Crow laughed. "For outlaws and chinks, huh?"

"Momma said there's lots of them in California. What the devil *is* a chink?"

"It's a Chinaman," Crow said.

"Oh . . . a Chinaman? You ever seen one?"

"Nope."

"I reckon walking to California is gonna take a while. You think we can make it, Crow?"

"I don't know. The frontier is a harsh place. Indians and wild animals and God only knows what else. Plenty have lost their lives on the frontier. It takes a savage breed to survive it."

"That's me! I'm a savage breed! Papa always said I was half rattlesnake and half fire ant, so I reckon that makes me a savage breed. I ain't scared of this adventure. If we can kill a bunch of demons, I guess we can kill pretty much anything that gets in our way."

"That reminds me," Crow said, "I was wondering what you said to Haggard when you knelt down beside him before he died. I saw you down there while I was reloading."

"Oh, I was just telling him his family was waiting for him in Heaven and that he done a good job fighting with us and that there weren't no hard feelings. You know, gushy shit like that."

"That was mighty kind of you."

"That's me!" Liz said. "Mighty kind!"

They walked on, as the sun rose high and then began descending, and as clouds and wind moved in, causing them to don their coats, and as coyotes howled to the north. They saw a large oak tree in the distance, standing alone on the prairie, with a ravine running not too far beyond. It would make a good camp for the night.

"You got anything to eat?" Liz Sawyer said,

looking down at the blood-stained handkerchief doll she had tucked in the pocket of her dress.

"Afraid not," said Crow, scratching at his tangled beard.

"Oh. Well, I'm hungry, and we're completely out of meat."

ABOUT THE AUTHOR

Patrick C. Harrison III (PC3, if you prefer) is an author of horror, bizarro, and erotica. His current publications include *Inferno Bound and the Hell Hounds*, *5 Tales That Will Land You in Hell*, *Visceral: Collected Flesh* with Christine Morgan, and *Cerberus Rising* with Chris Miller and M. Ennenbach, and his works can be found in numerous anthologies, including *And Hell Followed* and *Road Kill: Texas Horror by Texas Writers Vol. 4*.

PC3 is also the co-owner (with Jarod Barbee) and editor-in-chief of Death's Head Press, a Texas-based publisher of dark fiction. Some of the books DHP has edited and published over the last year-and-a-half include, *And Hell Followed*, *Breaking Bizarro*, *Dig Two Graves Vol. 1 & 2*, and *Obliquatur Voluptas: Deviant Stories for the Deviant Mind*.

PC3 is a family man at heart, who enjoys baseball, camping, horror movies, fishing, and, of course, reading. He lives in Wolfe City, TX with his wife and children.